NAT RIDLEY DETECTIVE STORIES

THE DOUBLE DAGGER

NAT RIDLEY DETECTIVE STORIES

THE DOUBLE DAGGER

or

Nat Ridley's Mexican Trail

By Nat Ridley, Jr.

Author of "Guilty or Not Guilty," "A Daring Abduction," "A Scream in the Dark," etc.

WILDSIDE PRESS

Originally published in 1926.
Published by Wildside Press LLC
wildsidepress.com

CHAPTER I

A CALL FOR HELP

With a vicious bang, which indicated that his thoughts were not on what he was doing, Nat Ridley hung the receiver on the telephone hook. He swung around in his swivel chair and looked out of the window of his Times Square office at the hurrying throngs converging at Broadway and Seventh Avenue.

"That's a new one, all right!" exclaimed the famous detective, more to himself than to anyone else, though Berry Todd, his capable assistant, was at a desk near by. "It sure is a new one! And to think that some of those human ants down there may have had a hand in it!"

He leaned forward the better to see out of the window.

"What's that?" asked Berry, who was shuffling over some papers. "Whose aunt are you talking about?"

"Nobody's aunt!" was Nat's reply. "I might just as well have said flies or bugs—that's what they look like!" He waved his hand to the hurrying throng—men and women mixed with automobiles.

"Oh—that bunch!" chuckled Berry. "Yes, there sure is a crowd. But is anything wrong?" he went on, for he realized that the mere sight of the crowd, almost always in evidence at this busy section of New York, was no new one for his chief. "Anything wrong?" asked Berry again, though in a lower voice, for he noted that the celebrated sleuth, whose exploits were the talk of two continents, was gazing abstractedly at the telephone.

"Yes, there is," snapped out Nat Ridley, though the crisp tone did not indicate impatience with his helper's insistence. "I can't quite make out why he should phone me."

"Who?" asked Berry, who was a privileged character.

"Carl Lemberg."

"That German sleuth?" cried Berry.

"He isn't as German as his name sounds," was Nat's reply. "Though of course he has many of the earmarks. But why he should want me to come in on one of his cases—"

"You don't mean to say he admits he's stuck, do you?" and Berry laughed. "That's pretty good! Lemberg up a blind alley—at the end of his trail—that's pretty good!"

The joke, if such it was, was all the more appreciated by Berry Todd, for of all the private detectives in New York, Nat Ridley's chief rival was this Carl Lemberg.

Yet Nat did not actually admit that Lemberg was a rival. It was only other detectives, some in the Ridley offices, who were thus bold about admitting the fact and, sometimes, complaining about it. For though the chief said nothing, more than once he had heard of some rather underhand practices on the part of Lemberg or the latter's helpers, practices that took from Nat Ridley cases that netted large sums of money.

But Nat Ridley was not one to complain, or even acknowledge that he had a rival. He took the cases that came to him, and not always for money, either. More than once he had worked day and night, and even endangered his life, solving a mystery for the very love of getting to the bottom of a tangle or for the sake of some friend.

Yet it could not be wholly ignored that Carl Lemberg was, in every sense of the word, a business rival of Nat Ridley's.

"So he's squealing, is he?" asked Berry. "What's the game? What sort of case has Lemberg that he can't solve, Chief?"

"He isn't exactly squealing, Berry," said Nat slowly, as he rose from his chair, pushed it back, and began nervously to pace the small private office. "He is in need of help."

"Then it's on a case, isn't it?" persisted Berry. "I'll bet a new straw hat, and the season's just opening, too," he added, "that he fell down on that Markwith jewelry robbery. They passed us up on that, Chief, and went to Lemberg. Now he's stuck! Serves him darn good and right!"

"No, it isn't the Markwith case, Berry," said Nat.

"What then?"

"It's a sort of family affair."

"Oh, a scandal? Well, we don't go in for that sort of thing, do we?"

"You haven't quite got me, Berry," and Nat smiled. "It isn't that kind of a case. Though it is a family matter for Lemberg. He's in need of help and he turns to me. Urgent need he said just now, over the telephone."

"Then it must be a big case!" declared Berry. "So much the better for us. I'd rather he'd be stuck on a big case and have to turn it over to us, than to have it a little jigger not worth bothering with. Want me to do anything, Chief?"

Nat Ridley slowly indicated a negative by a shake of his head.

"It hasn't gotten to that stage yet," he said. "In fact, I don't know what it is myself. I told him to come here and see me. Such matters aren't for the telephone."

"Then you're going to help him?"

This time Nat nodded in the affirmative.

"Whew!" whistled Berry Todd.

And there was reason for his surprise, for in addition to the rivalry existing between the two offices, there was a distinct feeling on Nat Ridley's part against Lemberg. The noted sleuth did not speak of this, but his friends and his office force knew of it.

Lemberg was too tricky, and Nat was out of sympathy with the manner in which the German, as he was often called, got some of his cases. And when Berry thought of that and heard his chief say he had agreed to listen to what Lemberg had to say, it is no wonder Berry whistled.

"Will he be here soon?" asked Berry, as he began to gather up the papers he was looking over. "If he will, I'd better light out. I was getting up the report for you on that kidnapping case, but—"

"Let it go, Berry," was the order. "Lemberg will be here in about five minutes, and he wants to see me alone. I'll let you and Baldy know what I decide to do."

"Lemberg will be here in five minutes?" exclaimed Berry as he put the papers in a portfolio and started for the door leading out of Nat's private room. "How's he coming—by air-ship?" The office of the other sleuth was down near Wall Street, several miles from Times Square.

"He is in our neighborhood," Nat went on. "He was so anxious to see me that he rode up here, and is down in the Grand Central Terminal now. He's coming up from there in a taxi."

"Well, I'll make myself scarce. But—you won't mind a word from an old friend as well as from one of your workers, Chief?" Berry seemed very anxious.

"Of course I won't!" declared Nat. "What is it?"

"Think twice before you have anything to do with Lemberg," was the low reply. "He's no better than a snake in the grass in my opinion."

"An opinion I quite agree with at times, Berry," was the rejoinder. "But I don't want to say I won't help him until I hear what he has to say. Judging from his voice, he was in quite a stew."

"Serves him right!" muttered Berry as he went out.

In a few minutes, during which Nat continued to pace the office, an electric buzzer near his desk signaled in a certain way.

"There he is!" murmured Nat, and, stepping to a button near the signal, he pressed it, indicating to Toodles, the office boy in the front office, that the chief would receive a visitor.

A moment later Carl Lemberg was ushered into Nat Ridley's private room.

In spite of the fact that he had lived all his life in the United States, there was a typical German appearance about this detective. He was massive in bulk and manner, and his voice, ordinarily, was loud and booming. It was this voice, more times than one, fairly hurled at a suspect, that had caused many to quail and confess.

Yet now Carl Lemberg was but a shadow of what he had been on occasions. Instead of entering the office with a firm and confident tread, he fairly slunk in, and he glanced from side to side, and once back of him, in a manner denoting that he feared he might have been followed.

His usually ruddy face was pale and his large hands trembled as he took a big linen handkerchief from his pocket and mopped his face.

"It is good of you to let me come, Ridley," began the visitor, with no trace of accent, though he spoke German fluently and with a purity seldom attained by those not born in Germany.

"I could do nothing less after what you said," rejoined the other. "What is the matter?"

"Much!" was the reply, and again came that nervous look about and behind. "Are we alone here?" he whispered.

"As much so as anyone is ever alone," was the reply, with a smile. "The walls are sound proof—as yours are."

"Oh, yes—mine—of course! And yet they haven't seemed to keep my secrets."

"What do you mean?" asked Nat.

"I—I wish I knew!" was the faltering reply. "I wish I knew!"

"Look here, Lemberg," exclaimed Nat with a brusk show of friendliness he did not altogether feel, "you're all in! You're showing fear! It may not be real, but—"

"I am afraid, Ridley! I am afraid!" was the quick reply. "I hardly dare admit to myself how frightened I am. That is why I have come to you."

"You? Afraid?" chuckled Nat, half scoffing. "I can't believe it."

"It's true, I tell you!" fairly snarled the other. "I am in deadly fear!"

"What of, in the name of all the police of New York?"

"I don't even know that. But it's terrible!"

There was no mistaking the man's terror. It showed in his voice, in his eyes, in his actions. Nat Ridley was astonished. To himself he murmured:

"The intrepid Carl Lemberg afraid? Am I dreaming?"

Aloud he said:

"You must have a reason for this fear. I suppose you came to tell me—to get my help. And, if so—"

"Yes! Yes!" broke in the other detective. "You are ready to laugh at me, I know. I feel it! I would not be surprised. Yet, you would be afraid also if —"

He paused, startled by some noise unperceived by Nat.

"Well, what?" suggested the other. "I would be afraid if what?"

8

"If your brother had been murdered, and then your uncle and then your chief assistant. I ask you, Nat Ridley, if you would not, also, have fear under those circumstances? Would you—?"

At that instant the telephone on the desk jingled out an imperative summons, and, coming, as it did, at such a dramatic moment, even Nat Ridley was startled.

CHAPTER II

THE DOUBLE DAGGER

For a moment or two the telephone bell continued to sound its summons, and both men stared at it. The German detective made a motion as though to answer, and then, recollecting that he was not in his own office, he stepped back with a mutter of impatience.

"Excuse me," murmured Nat as he picked up the instrument.

"Certainly."

To Nat's ears came the voice of Berry Todd in the latter's office near the entrance to the sleuth's suite.

"All right, Chief?" asked Berry in guarded tones.

"All right about what?" Nat countered, for he did not get the drift of the other's question.

Berry went on with:

"Excuse me, Chief, but I happened to notice that bird sliding into your office, and I didn't like his looks. No names, you understand, but I thought he looked desperate, and he might have suddenly gone batty, you know, and might try to slip you a bomb, or something like that. How about it? Need any help? Are you all right?"

"All right," Nat answered, hardly able to keep from chuckling at the odd thought Berry had given voice to. The sleuth, who was very fond of his chief in more than a business way, had noted, with more than a little apprehension, the entrance of Lemberg.

Indeed Lemberg was acting very queerly, but Nat Ridley was not afraid for himself, though he appreciated Berry's precaution.

"Quite all right," said Nat again, as he put the receiver on the hook. "Sorry to have had to interrupt you," he went on to his visitor. "But, being in the same line of business—"

"Oh, of course—yes. Perhaps I shouldn't have come in. But I could not stand it any longer. Though if you have an urgent case—"

"There wouldn't seem to be any more urgent than your own," said Nat. "This was only one of my men reporting. I am quite ready to hear you further. Did I understand you to say that your brother and uncle had been murdered?"

"That's it—foully murdered, Ridley! And now Dan Steele—"

"What?" cried Nat, startled out of his usual calmness. "You don't mean to tell me Steele has been killed? How? When? Where? Why, Dan used to work for me at one time."

"I know he did. A fine chap he is—was, I mean. When I got word that the devils had put the sign on him I decided it was too much for me to handle. And, knowing you had once hired Steele, I decided to come to you."

"You had better sit down and tell me about it," suggested Nat, for, up to this time, Lemberg had been pacing the office.

"It is a long story, but I will make it as short as possible," he said, as he slumped, rather than sat, in a chair. Again he mopped his pale and perspiring face. "You may not know it," went on Lemberg, "but I am in the oil-well business."

"I had not heard it," stated Nat. "The venture must have been recently made."

"It was. I would not have gone into it had not these murders forced it upon me. For years, as you know, I have conducted a private detective agency, just as you have."

Nat did not quite like the simile, for he would not admit that he conducted the same sort of business as had Carl Lemberg. But Nat let that pass, and the other went on:

"My brother, Henry, and my uncle, August, some years ago bought the rights to several valuable oil properties in the neighborhood of Rolamotaza, in Mexico. The wells turned out better than was expected, and my uncle and brother decided to increase their holdings.

"Near their property were some wells belonging to a number of Mexicans, who formed a sort of corporation for marketing the product they pumped out of the earth. As is natural, where natural products are so close together, there were frequent quarrels over mineral rights, and matters got to such a point that my uncle and brother decided they would either have to buy out their rivals or sell to them.

"Finally it settled to a matter of the former, and a deal was made by which the Mexican firm transferred their rights, titles and interests to my two relatives. The Mexicans were paid a large sum, all they had demanded, as a matter of fact, and, getting the money, they disappeared."

Lemberg paused again to mop his face.

"Nothing very remarkable in all this, so far," said Nat, who had been jotting down some pencil characters on a paper. This had been observed by his visitor who sharply asked:

"What are you doing?"

"Taking shorthand notes."

"Have you no stenographer?" the German inquired.

"Yes," and Nat smiled. "But there are some things I do not trust even to my own stenographer. Proceed, if you please. You have yet to come to the murders."

"I will come to them—never fear!" declared the other earnestly. "As I said, the Mexicans, after their wells were bought, disappeared, but some time later they came back."

"Why?"

"Because the properties they sold to my brother and uncle turned out to be much more valuable than had been thought. In other words, much oil began to spout in wells it was thought were running dry, and, as a result, my uncle and brother began to grow very wealthy."

"And the Mexicans came back, I suppose," said Nat, "to get a share of it?"

"Exactly. But as my relatives had paid all that was asked, and as they had no knowledge that the wells would turn out better than was supposed, they did not see why they should pay over any of their profits."

"No, as a business proposition, they couldn't be expected to," Nat agreed.

"And then came the murders!" exclaimed Lemberg suddenly.

"How?" cried Nat.

"One night, after several veiled threats had been made against my two relatives, my brother Henry was found dead—there was a dagger in his heart!"

"The Latin races run to knives," murmured Nat.

"A few days after that," went on Lemberg, "and following the receipt by my uncle of an anonymous threat that if he did not share some of his oil wealth with the former owners of the wells he would be killed, he, too, was found dead."

"Murdered?"

"Murdered!"

"With a dagger?"

"With a dagger, just as my brother had been, and with the same sign."

"What do you mean—with the same sign?"

"This!" and the German sleuth took a little package from his coat pocket. He opened it and spread the contents on Nat's desk. There were two dirty cards, on one of which were tell-tale red stains, and each card bore on one side the drawing, crudely done, of a double dagger.

The weapon seemed to consist of a middle handle, made of some sort of twisted horn, or perhaps hard wood. One of the blades of the double dagger was longer than the other, and both points were shown very keen in the picture.

"Rather an odd weapon," commented Nat, taking up one of the cards by the edges so as to leave no finger prints on those presumably already there. "I think I have seen it before. Just a moment."

He turned to a large book case and opened the glass door.

"What are you going to do?" asked Lemberg.

"Look up this symbol—for a symbol I think it is."

"You are right," said the other. "As I said, it is a sign. But here is one of the daggers," and from another pocket Lemberg took a small box which he turned upside down on Nat's desk.

There was a metallic sound, and there tinkled out on the shining oak a small dagger, exactly like the pictured one on the card, but so small as to be useless as a weapon.

"It looks like a pin," commented Nat Ridley.

"It was used as a pin," the German said. "With these pins these cards were fastened to the clothing of my brother and my uncle."

"I see," murmured Nat. He reached forward to pick up the murderous little implement, but Lemberg caught his hand.

"The points may be poisoned," was the caution.

"They may be," admitted Nat. "I was going to exercise due caution, Lemberg," he added, with a grim laugh. "But did your uncle and brother die from the scratch of a poisoned weapon?"

"They may have, for all I know to the contrary, though from the report of the police in Rolamotaza the cuts in their hearts brought death. If there was poison used, it was to make assurance doubly sure. But it is best to be cautious."

"You are right. So the cards, bearing the picture of this dagger, were fastened on the dead men's clothing with pins made in the same shape. Were the heart stabs made by the same sort of daggers, only larger?"

"That is the supposition. But I can save you time, Ridley. You were going to look up this symbol?"

"Yes," admitted Nat. "I have some books on foreign secret societies. I think I recognize this symbol. It is, I am sure—"

"The Tola," interrupted Lemberg. "I looked it up. Yes, it is an old Mexican society, but it was supposed to have died out years ago."

"Then it has revived," stated Nat.

"Or else it never died. Well, to get on with my story. When I got word of my brother's death, I started the police in Mexico after the murderers. They did what they could—little enough—and while I was waiting their report, my uncle went the same way.

"Then I acted quickly, and sent my best man down to Paloma, Texas, with orders to cross into Mexico and see if he could round up these oil-well killers."

"He went, I suppose?" suggested Nat.

Lemberg bowed gravely.

"But he never came back," he said. "Dan Steele was murdered in Paloma in the same way my brother and uncle had been killed—with a dagger thrust in his heart, and this card pinned on his breast. Do you wonder I am afraid, Ridley?"

"Not after that," was the answer. "But what form does your fear take?"

"A fear for myself. I have reason to believe they will kill me next—those mysterious murderers of the Tola!" and, with a shaking hand, Carl Lemberg again mopped his face.

CHAPTER III

ANOTHER MURDER

Nat Ridley was accustomed to seeing strong men exhibit fear under many circumstances. Sometimes it was a fear over the consequences of the crimes the detective had fastened on them. Again it might be a fear over the outcome of some fight about to take place—a fight with revolvers or daggers. More seldom he had seen clients of his exhibit terror under just such circumstances as now confronted him—fear of vengeance from some cause.

"But I never," declared Nat, telling of the matter later to his two assistants, Berry Todd and Baldy Stoler, "saw a man in such a state of fear as Lemberg was."

Realizing, as he sat there facing the German sleuth, who, as a last resort, had applied to a rival for aid, Nat Ridley realized that he must say or do something to reassure Lemberg.

"If I don't, he may have a nervous breakdown in my office and make an unpleasant sensation," decided the great detective.

Accordingly, Nat strode over to where Lemberg was sitting in a chair, and fairly trembling now. He placed a firm hand on the German's powerful shoulder—Lemberg would have made two Nat Ridley figures, with something left over—and exclaimed sternly:

"Look here, now! Don't make a fool of yourself, Lemberg! You arc in no immediate danger. You are safe in my office. Pull yourself together. No one can harm you here, and if I am to help you I must have more particulars. You are in no danger here."

"I—I am not so sure of that," whispered the German, looking nervously around and out of the windows. "This Tola gang is terrible!"

"They may be. I know, from reading their history, that they were a blood-thirsty offshoot of the Aztecs," admitted Nat. "But they can't get you here!"

"Dan Steele thought they couldn't get him," said Lemberg in a low voice. "But they did! And after my brother's murder and my uncle had received mysterious warnings to leave the country, he boasted that they couldn't get him. But they did! And now I think they will get me."

"But why?" asked Nat. "You aren't down there in Mexico. You're in the heart of New York."

"And some of the Tolas may be in this very building!" declared the German sleuth.

"What object would they have in killing you, granted that they have some of their agents in New York?" Nat wanted to know.

"As the heir of my uncle and brother, I inherit most of those oil wells," was the answer. "Their enmity will run against me now, unless I relinquish my claim. I am going to do that, only I fear it will be too late. Vengeance may already be sworn against me."

"Nonsense!" Nat said, with a short laugh. He was trying to make his visitor forget some of his fear. "The wells are legally yours. Why should you give them up? Especially when it well may be that these fellows are scoundrels—that they are just playing on your fears to get you to give in. The wells were bought and paid for, and you are entitled to them."

Lemberg shook his ponderous head, and remarked:

"It seems that the Tola society, or the present-day members of it, want money from the wells to re-establish their ancient splendor and power. They want to make the Tola what it was in the days of the Spanish Conquistadores. My uncle and brother did not know, when they bought the wells, that the land, centuries ago, was owned by the Tolas. Now they want it back again."

"How did you learn this?" asked Nat.

"From the reports Steele sent in before he was killed."

"Where are those reports now?"

"In my office."

"I should like to look at them," said Nat with interest—"that is, if I am to help you in this matter."

"Oh, but you will help me, won't you, Ridley?" gasped Lemberg, seizing the detective's hand. "I need help, and I don't know where to turn but to you! See if you can't run these criminals down—find out where they are hiding. Tell them I'll give back the wells if they will only let me sleep in peace at night. I'm a wreck!"

Indeed the man looked it. There were big, puffy bags under his eyes, and his hands trembled.

"But why did they kill Dan Steele?" asked Nat. "He had no interest in the mines, did he?"

"No. I sent him to Mexico to run down the gang, and he was hot on their trail when the double dagger got him. Poor Dan!"

"Poor Dan is right!" echoed Nat. "I knew him well. He was a friend of mine, and for his sake—to avenge him—I'm going to take this case, Lemberg."

"Thank you for that, Ridley!" exclaimed the other fervently. "It will take a load off my mind. But be careful of yourself. Once it is known you are seeking the Tola gang—those who carry the symbol of the double dagger—your life may pay the forfeit."

"I've been threatened before," replied Nat grimly.

"But never in this way!" and Lemberg's voice was very serious. "Once they find out you are working against them to help me—to avenge the murders of my brother and uncle—they will—"

"They will not find out I am working on the case," interrupted Nat Ridley. "I've dealt with fellows like this before."

"You don't know them!" warned Lemberg. "I took a roundabout way in riding to your office, but I fear I was followed. I doubled on my tracks and made a twisting trail, but I still fear I was followed."

"Well, we'll see that they don't see you leaving here," Nat promised. "I have means of getting from this room to the floor above and down a rear freight elevator that will fool the cleverest stalker. Don't worry about that, nor about me. Now let's get down to brass tacks. Tell me everything you can."

For an hour or more Carl Lemberg related all the details of the triple crime, and Nat made shorthand notes, to the no small admiration of his fellow sleuth, who declared it was a valuable adjunct to Nat's talents. At the end of the talk Nat said:

"I must go over Steele's reports. There may be something in them that you have forgotten."

"Very likely there is," admitted Lemberg. "I'm in such a state that at times I hardly know what I am doing. If you will come to my office you shall see all the papers."

Nat made an appointment for that afternoon, and then escorted the German out of the office by a special stairway leading to the floor above, so he could get out by a freight entrance.

"Don't worry," advised Nat as he shook hands with Lemberg. "They won't spot you leaving here. And I think it is mostly your imagination that is causing your fears."

"It is no imagination!" declared Lemberg, fervently.

However, he seemed to have gotten safely away from Nat's Times Square office, for the sleuth sent Baldy down to Broadway to make sure nothing happened, and the old detective reported that Lemberg had "scurried into a taxicab like a rabbit in the hunting season."

"What's it all about, Chief?" asked Baldy, with the freedom of an old retainer.

"You and Berry might as well hear the outlines of the case, and Mary Dotley, also," remarked the sleuth, naming his clever woman detective. "If

I am going to take it, and I have promised Lemberg that I will, you may be called on to lend a hand now and then. Come in and I'll go over it with you."

The story of the Tola murders was told briefly, and Nat showed the card, bearing the device of the double dagger, and also the little weapon that was used as a pin.

"I want you to take this pin to Professor Watson, of Columbia University, and have him analyze it for possible poison," said Nat to Berry at the end of the conference. "And be careful you don't scratch yourself with the point."

"I'm wise," declared Berry. "But suppose you do find it poisoned?"

"It may give me a line on the scoundrels who are using it and who have killed three men," said Nat. "Those ancient Aztecs were devils in more ways than one, and maybe the Tolas have inherited some of their cunning and kept alive some of their knowledge."

While Berry went to the university laboratory, Nat, after going over some matters in his office and starting his other assistants on the new cases that had come in, went to Lemberg's suite of rooms in a building on lower Broadway.

Though the sleuth rather discounted the fears of the German, yet Nat was taking no chances. So he adopted a suitable disguise, in the art of which he was a master, and was also very careful how he approached the building where the German detective had his offices.

Nat looked carefully about as he approached the entrance, and his keen eyes searched every face. Not until he was satisfied that he was not being shadowed, did he enter.

He found Lemberg nervously pacing the floor and waiting for him.

"Ah, you are come! It is good!" exclaimed the German. "Now you shall read what devils they are!"

He spread out on a desk the various reports Dan Steele had sent in from Rolamotaza, the town nearest the Mexican oil wells. The first reports contained little but routine matters, but as Dan remained longer in the place he began to uncover some queer information about some queer characters.

"It begins to look a little more promising," commented Nat, glancing up from the reports.

"Yes," agreed Lemberg. "But read on."

Nat read, coming to the bottom paper in the pile, where Dan wrote that he was going out to a certain place where, he had reason to believe, the Tola gang held secret meetings. Nat read to the end of this report and looked up.

"Where are the others?" he asked.

"What others?"

"The other papers—the rest of the report."

"There are no more," Lemberg sadly answered. "Dan Steele never came back after writing that. He went to his death!"

Even the stoical Nat Ridley was startled at hearing this. But he shook off for the time what sentiment gripped him and bent to the business in hand. He made copious notes of all Steele had reported on, and then definitely announced to Lemberg that he would at once begin work on the case.

"And may you track down the murderers!" exclaimed the German. "I shall sleep a little sounder to-night from knowing that you have this case, Nat Ridley."

"Yes, Lemberg, I'll do my best. And I hope you do sleep soundly. I will see you to-morrow and make further arrangements."

Nat bid the other detective good-day and hurried back to his own office, using the same precautions as before. It was early afternoon, and he had several matters to clear off his desk before going into the Mexican puzzle. For three hours Nat was kept busy.

It was about five o'clock, and nearly time for Nat's office to close, when Tommy Ray, or more popularly "Toodles," the office boy, came rushing into the office, having gone to the street to get a paper for Miss Dotley. Tommy's face showed great excitement, so much so that Nat Ridley, coming out of his office for a moment, noted it and asked:

"What's up, Toodles—did the Giants lose?"

"Look!" gasped the lad, holding out a paper across the front page of which, in big letters were the words:

MURDERED IN A TAXI

"Well, there's nothing new in that," commented Nat as he held out his hand to glance at the sheet a moment.

"Wait until you see who it is!" Tommy exclaimed. He pointed to a name in the first paragraph of the story.

"Carl Lemberg!" gasped Nat, shaken out of his calm. "Why, I was in his office only a few hours ago!"

Nat read hurriedly how the well-known detective had been stabbed through the heart while riding home from his office in a taxicab.

"I've got to get busy on this right away!" cried Nat, as he tossed the paper back to Tommy. "Lemberg killed, just as he feared he would be! The Tolas got him!"

CHAPTER IV

AN ORDER TO RAMON

From the hasty perusal of the flash story in the paper, Nat Ridley gained an idea of how Lemberg had met his death—that is, he knew all the police had found out in the short time between the discovery of the body in the cab and the issuing of the evening extra.

"Look after matters here until I get back, Berry," called Nat to his assistant. "I'm going to have a look in that taxi."

"Right!" Berry assented. "If you need any help phone in."

"I will. And, Berry—" Nat spoke in a lower tone, though there was no one else in his office, "just keep your eyes open."

"For anything special, Chief?"

"For a sight of any men who look as if they might be Mexicans or Spaniards," was Nat's reply. "I'm off!" and he hurried to catch one of the descending elevators in the corridor.

The story of the murder of Lemberg, as set out briefly in the paper, was to the effect that the chauffeur of the cab drove his fare to the address given him, which was a German club where the detective made it a habit to dine several times a week. The driver, finding that his passenger did not alight on arrival, looked around to see what caused the delay.

"I saw the gentleman sort of slumped over like, in his seat," the taxi man told the police. "I thought maybe he had been hitting up the bootleg. But when I shook him, I saw he was covered with blood. There was a lot of it on his vest and there was a hole, right over his heart. I called a cop from the next corner and he got the ambulance. That's all I know."

The story went on to say that Lemberg was dead when taken to Bellevue Hospital, and the surgeon who examined the detective said he had died instantly from a stab wound in the heart.

There was no weapon found in the cab, and the first theory of suicide was passed over when the surgeon said no man could have given himself such a deadly wound.

"The question is," said Nat to himself as he made his way to the nearest police station where, so the paper said, the taxi and driver had been taken for examination after the body was removed, "when was Lemberg stabbed? Obviously, some time between getting into the cab near his office and where it drew up at the curb in front of his club. I must have a talk with Carter, the taxi man."

Nat had no difficulty getting all the information he wanted from the New York police. Though a private detective, Nat had more than once given the regular force valuable clews on cases other than his own.

"Whatever in reason Nat Ridley wants, let him have," had been the standing orders of Inspector Rossberg of the metropolitan force.

"Hello, Kelly!" called Nat on entering the station house and nodding to the lieutenant behind the desk. Then, not to make it appear that he had come around especially to find out more about the strange murder, Nat went on: "You haven't seen Baldy around this afternoon, have you?"

"No, Mr. Ridley, I haven't," was the answer. "Is he in this neighborhood?"

"He might be," was Nat's noncommittal answer.

Baldy Stoler was well known to Lieutenant Kelly and to others of the regular New York police, since he had been on the force before leaving to join Nat's agency.

"Working on a case, I suppose?" went on Kelly.

"That's it. I thought maybe he might have dropped in here as this would be on his way. But I guess it's too late now. Anything new?"

It was a stereotyped question, such as Nat often asked, but this time he knew what the answer would be.

"Well, yes," Kelly replied slowly. "We have a bit of a case here—it might be in your line, too."

"A case?" questioned Nat, as though he had no idea in the world what was coming next. "What sort?"

"Murder."

"Oh, they're common enough," and the sleuth spoke with an air of indifference. "I hardly think it will interest me, unless it is out of the ordinary."

"That's just it!" declared Kelly, with a chuckle. "It's very extraordinary, or I wouldn't have mentioned it to you. And it concerns a friend of yours— or rather, a rival."

"What's the joke?" asked Nat, as he lighted one of his strong, black cigars and passed one like it to the appreciative officer.

"No joke at all, Mr. Ridley. There's been a mysterious murder done in the last hour and the man killed is Carl Lemberg, the private detective. You know him, don't you?"

"Sure! You don't mean to tell me he's dead!" and Nat was sufficiently startled to throw Kelly off the track. Whereupon the lieutenant proceeded to give details, adding that the taxi was even then in the garage of the police station and the driver was in Captain Flood's room being questioned.

"You don't tell me!" and Nat continued to be astonished. "Do they suspect the driver?"

"Oh, no! He's out of it. Here he comes now," and, as Kelly spoke, the precinct commander emerged from his private office, followed by a typical New York taxi driver. The fellow looked anxious and worried, but his face cleared as the captain, after nodding to Nat, said:

"It's all right, Kelly. This man can go. I know where to get him when I want him. He hasn't the least bit of evidence. Report here once a day until this affair is over, Carter," said the captain crisply.

"Yes, sir. And can I take my cab along?"

"Well, no, not just yet," was the answer. But as the man's face fell, the captain said: "I'll arrange with the taxi company to let you have another machine. We may need this for evidence."

"Oh, all right," and Carter's face cleared again. He left the station house and Nat talked with the captain, mentioning what Kelly had told him about Lemberg.

"A queer case," said the commander. "In broad daylight, on one of the busiest streets in the world, a man is stabbed in a taxi and the murderer gets away. Fierce, I call it! The papers will pound us again."

"You've got to expect that," answered Nat Ridley, with a grim smile. "But how does this taxi man account for not hearing anything?"

"The only way he says it might have happened was when he was caught in a traffic jam soon after picking up his fare. There was some blasting being done, to put down a foundation for a new building, and the street was blocked off a minute or two. The driver thinks that Lemberg was stabbed just at the blast went off, which would have prevented his cries being heard or any noise of the struggle coming out of the cab."

"The murderer picked a good time," commented Nat. "But how did he get into the cab?"

"That's something Carter doesn't know. Lemberg may have been followed up by someone who had a grudge against him. You know he has shown up some pretty big bootleggers and dope peddlers. Well, one of them may have been laying in wait and hopped into the cab just as, or soon after, Lemberg got in. He could have chloroformed the German, or maybe kept him quiet by a threat, and, when the blast came, he might have driven the knife in. It is also possible that when the cab stopped, on account of the traffic jam, that then the murderer opened the door and did the trick, the blast covering Lemberg's call for help."

"That sounds more reasonable than the other," said Nat. "Well, it isn't any of my affair."

"I'm going out to look in the cab," said the captain. "Some of my men have given it the once over, but I always like to take a peep for myself.

Want to come?"

"I might, since I can't locate Baldy," stated Nat, as if it was of no moment.

A little later he was standing in a quiet street at the rear of the police station and garage. The taxicab had been driven out into the open and was standing there.

"He bloodied it up a bit," commented the captain as he opened the door. "They'll have to put new leather on before they can run this out again," and he indicated several dark red stains. "But there doesn't seem to be much else," he added as he looked carefully over the interior of the vehicle. "Guess we'll have to get the finger-print experts down here. Yes, Duffy, what is it?" he asked as a patrolman, whom Nat knew slightly, came out and stood waiting for his superior.

"You're wanted on the phone, sir," Duffy reported. "It's Inspector Rossberg about that bond robbery."

"Oh, I'll be right in. See you later, Ridley. This isn't your case, but look around if you like."

"Thanks," rejoined Nat, and he peered into the cab. Almost at once a fleck of something white between the back and the seat cushions caught the detective's eyes. He looked around and noted that Duffy was engaged in lighting a cigar, and then, with a quick motion, Nat put his hand between the cushions and pulled out the white object.

He could hardly restrain an exclamation of surprise when he saw that it was a card, and scrawled on it was the device of the double dagger!

"I might have known it would be here!" thought Nat. "The Mexicans were on Lemberg's trail, and they got him. Bold devils they are! Knifing him in a taxi in broad daylight in the heart of New York!"

He shot another glance at Duffy, but the patrolman, who was on reserve duty, was taking advantage of the chance to get some fresh air and was strolling about in the neighborhood of the taxi.

With a quick motion Nat Ridley slipped the card into his pocket and was about to walk away when he noticed three men strolling along the street and curiously observing the vehicle. The men had dark, swarthy complexions, their hair was black, sleek, and shiny and their dark eyes were shifty.

"Mexicans or Spaniards, if I'm any judge!" mused Nat. "And it wouldn't surprise me in the least to learn that they came along to find out just what the police are going to do in this murder case. I wish I knew more about them. I will, soon. Meanwhile—"

Just then Duffy strolled over toward Nat and did exactly what the detective wished should not happen. For the patrolman greeted the sleuth loudly by name, and added:

"You working on this taxicab murder?"

"No, Duffy, I'm not!" said Nat decidedly. "I have other fish to fry. I'm as busy as all get-out on another case. I have no time to look into this. Besides, I think it's a case of suicide."

"No! Do you now?" asked the policeman. "Well, maybe 'twas. Thim Germans are great for suicidin'. I wouldn't put it past this fellow, though I didn't know him. So you're not on it?"

"No, Duffy. I just stopped in out of idle curiosity. It doesn't interest me in the least."

"Well, I guess the regular police detectives will find out about it," went on Duffy with the ordinary policeman's faith in the wisdom of the sleuths. "Comin' in?" he asked.

"No, I'm off," Nat answered.

The talk, on his part, had been purposely loud. He had noted with some alarm the lingering walk of the three dark-skinned men. They seemed to want to remain in the vicinity of the taxicab to hear what was being said.

"If they can make anything out of what I said they're welcome," muttered Nat to himself as he prepared to walk along.

But he caught a glimpse of the face of one of the trio, and on that face was a sneer. It was as though the dark fellow had been laughing—as though he was not in the least deceived by the effort Nat Ridley had made to throw off suspicion. If the strangers knew the name Ridley, they could not have failed to have heard Duffy's loud use of it.

Then the sneering man spoke, giving a sharp order to his righthand companion. Though he may have been speaking of someone else, Nat Ridley had a strong suspicion that he himself was the one referred to when the sneerer said:

"Ramon, you shall watch that pig! I do not trust him nor any of them! Watch him!"

"He shall be watched, Señor," was the low-voiced reply as Ramon received his orders. And Nat Ridley caught Ramon flash a look at him that boded no good.

CHAPTER V

THE ROPE IN THE DARK

"Now just what?" mused Nat Ridley to himself, as the three dark-featured men sauntered on their way. "What does that mean? No good, I'm positive. But were they referring to me or to someone else?"

The detective, now that he had decided to enter this mysterious case, determined to do his best, not only to avenge a fellow practitioner, but for the sake of his own reputation. That is, his reputation as regarded by himself. He cared little for what the public thought or said, did Nat Ridley. But it was something to make a good, clean clearing up of a case for the sake of himself and those in his office. So it was a matter of pride with the sleuth not to be beaten in this battle of murder and wits.

"If I challenge them," reasoned Nat, "and accuse them of speaking of me as a pig, I shall lay myself open to the charge of butting in on somebody else's business. That might queer matters at the start."

Therefore he decided against that, but as he watched the men walking slowly away he mentally photographed their features in his memory so that he would know them again. And not only did he make a lasting vision of the men's faces, but of their walk, their actions, and such of their peculiarities as appeared on the surface.

"For if they are what I think they are, they'll use disguises the next time I see them," reasoned Nat. "They must have spotted me all right, though how, I don't know."

On the other hand, Nat realized that he might be on the wrong track, that these men might be idle, curious individuals who had heard about the murder—as who had not by this time?

"And they could easily claim, if I talked with them, that they were speaking of one of their own acquaintances when they used the endearing term of pig," chuckled Nat. "Well, what's the next move, I wonder?"

And wondering this, the detective also wondered whether, by the talk he had indulged in with Duffy, he had or had not thrown the dark-featured men off the track.

"First of all," decided the sleuth, "I'll have a go at those fellows. No use letting them get away with anything. I'll shadow them and see where they hang out."

It was the work of but a few moments for him to slip into a sheltered corner where he made some quick changes in his clothing and appearance, so that when he emerged and took up the trail of the trio, Nat Ridley resembled anything but the efficient officer who, a little while before, had been peering into the murder taxi.

The three Mexicans—Nat decided they were of that nationality—strolled along, talking in Spanish, as the sleuth made certain by catching a few words that floated back to him. He knew something of the language, though not much.

The trio appeared to be in no hurry, and evidently did not suspect that they were being followed, for they did not use any of the ordinary devices to confuse a trailer. Nor did they look back.

When they were a few blocks away from the police station and the cab in which Carl Lemberg had been slain, the Mexicans hailed a passing taxi.

"They're in a hurry," decided Nat who was not far behind the three. He quickly looked around for another taxi that he might use for himself, but saw none that was empty and he had a vision of being left behind. Then he noticed a small delivery wagon from one of New York's big department stores. The driver was a young man and Nat signaled to him.

For a moment the young fellow seemed to think it was a case of being held up in broad daylight, and he was about to step on the gas as he neared Nat when the latter called:

"I'm a secret service man chasing some crooks. I need your help."

"Oh, that's different," and a relieved look came over the lad's face. "I thought you were a stick-up man. But I haven't got anything, anyhow. What's the dope?"

"Follow that taxi—that is, if you can spare the time," begged Nat, showing his shield. "If not, drive along until I meet a cruising cab."

"I've got time," was the answer. "I'm through for the day."

And with such speed and skill did he follow the cab containing the three Mexicans that he was not far behind them when their vehicle halted in front of the Club Tamalle, a resort frequented by Spaniards.

"This is what I want to know," said Nat as he slipped the young fellow a two-dollar bill. "Much obliged."

"Are they counterfeiters?" the lad asked, with a smile, as he pocketed the money.

"Maybe that, and worse," answered Nat. "Just keep still about what happened just now."

"That's what I will. I hope you get them."

"I will!" declared Nat.

He waited until the three entered the club, which was at its liveliest later at night, and then got out of the delivery auto. Using that, instead of another taxi, to chase his quarry had enabled Nat to fool them completely, he thought.

He slipped over to the nearest subway and went back to his office with the mysterious card he had taken from the crack between the back and the seat cushions of the taxi in which Lemberg had breathed his last.

It was now early evening, but Berry Todd was on duty in the office, having sent out to get some sandwiches while waiting for Nat's return or for some word from the chief.

"Anything doing?" the younger sleuth greeted his employer.

"I think so," was the answer. "Get out the magnifying glasses, Berry, and the finger-print records. This card may show something," and Nat carefully laid the bit of pasteboard on a clean sheet of paper. "Any report from Columbia about that little dagger?" he asked.

"It came in over the phone a few minutes ago," was the reply. "It isn't a deadly poison on the points of the pin shaped like a dagger, but it is some kind of dope that numbs a person."

"That accounts for it!" exclaimed Nat. "They must prick or scratch their victim with that, and so render him helpless—so he can't yell—then they knife him! We're coming on. Now for some finger-print work."

Though the card bore several different finger or thumb prints, they were those of persons not registered in the books of criminals on file in Nat Ridley's office.

"Well, whoever handled this card hasn't yet been finger-printed around here," decided Nat when the test was over. "I'll have to get in touch with headquarters and some of the international books to-morrow. But I've got another job on hand now."

"You don't mean to say you're going to keep on with this case now, do you?" objected Berry. "You haven't had supper!"

"Well, I'm going to get a bite, and then I'm going to see Mrs. Lemberg —the widow of the murdered man. She may be able to throw some light on why he was killed. But you needn't stay, Berry. Lock up the office."

A little later, having again changed his disguise to that of a care-free man about town, Nat called on Carl Lemberg's widow. Mrs. Lemberg lived in the Bronx, and Nat found with her Anna Lemberg, the sister of the dead detective.

Both women showed traces of their grief when Nat was ushered into their apartment, having sent up his card which brought a ready invitation to come up.

"It is very good of you to come," said Mrs. Lemberg. "My husband often spoke of you, and said, after poor Dan Steele was killed, that he was going to engage you."

"He did engage me, and no later than to-day," stated Nat. "But he should have been a bit sooner, it appears."

"Yes, they—they got him!" muttered the sister. "Tell me," and her blue eyes sparkled dangerously, "do you know who the scoundrels were? Have you any trace of them?"

"It is a little too soon for that," Nat answered gently. "But I am going to do my best. I came to see if you could throw any light on this mystery."

"We will tell you all we know," promised Mrs. Lemberg. "But, unfortunately, it isn't much. My husband seldom brought his office affairs home."

However, she and Miss Anna brought out some papers from the desk of the dead detective, and Nat delved into them. Some of the things he discovered seemed to give him satisfaction, for he smiled in a grim way as he made some notes in his book. Then he questioned the two women closely, and learned a bit more.

"Well," the detective said finally, as he prepared to leave, "I think it looks a little more hopeful than it did at first."

"You mean you think you can find the murderers?" asked Anna.

"I hope so. At least, I can make a start and perhaps get on their trail, though where it will lead, no one can say. I may have to go to Mexico."

"Oh, I hope not!" exclaimed Mrs. Lemberg.

"Why not?" asked Nat, with a quick look at her.

"Because I fear it means death," she answered simply. "Look what happened to my husband's brother and his uncle. If only they had not gone there!"

"But they had business there," said Nat.

"Yes, I know. And then Mr. Steele went, and they killed him. My husband talked of going—only talked, mind you—and see what happened to him!"

"It does seem a sinister place," admitted Nat. "But forewarned is forearmed, you know. If I go to Mexico I will be on my guard. I may call to see you again," were his parting words.

The widow, as she escorted him to the door, said again:

"Whatever happens, don't go to Mexico!"

Something appeared to have happened to the street lights, for when the detective emerged from the Lemberg apartment the thoroughfare was in considerable darkness, the only illumination coming from stores and residences along the way.

But Nat thought little of this as he started off toward the nearest subway, intending to go to his home on Central Park West, to spend the night.

There was a dark alley midway in the block along which Nat Ridley was walking, his thoughts busy with the strange happenings of the day. But if he saw this dark side passage he gave it little thought until he heard a peculiar hissing sound coming from it.

"A snake!" thought Nat instantly, for that is exactly what it sounded like. He gave a momentary thought to the possibility that one of the big pythons from the Bronx Zoölogical Park might have escaped and be hiding in the dark alley.

The next instant he felt some thin, but powerful, coils circling about his neck. For an instant the iron nerve of the sleuth almost failed, and he put up his hands to ward off what he thought were the folds of a serpent.

Then, in the dark, he felt the coils of a rope. An instant later the noose was pulled tight, almost choking him, and he was hauled backward, pulled off his feet, and dragged in the silent and gloomy alley.

CHAPTER VI

A CHANGE OF IDENTITIES

"Pronto!"

The word was hissed out in the darkness from somewhere behind Nat Ridley as he was roughly pulled deeper into the alley.

Struggling as he was to keep the coils from choking him into insensibility by their constriction, the detective kept his wits enough to remember that this word was Spanish for "hurry" or "quick."

"The Tolas are after me, or someone they think I am," mused Nat grimly. "They're fast workers—must have followed me to the Lemberg apartment and been on the watch. Wonder if they put out the street lamps. No, they couldn't have done that. Must have been just an accident that favored them."

These thoughts rushed like lightning through the detective's brain as he nerved himself for the struggle he knew must follow.

Come the fight did, an instant later. Nat succeeded in forcing up over his head the coils of the lasso, and only just in time, for it was tightening cruelly. But meanwhile, he had been hauled by the rope deeper into the dark alley, so that now he was several yards from the street whence help might come.

"We have him—the pig!" a voice grunted, as Nat felt strong arms about him, and he recognized the tones as those of one of the three men who had used the same expression that afternoon.

"The knife—pronto!" exclaimed another, and Nat knew they meant to kill him as Lemberg had been killed—even as Steele and the others had been murdered. Then a fierce, fighting rage took possession of Nat Ridley and he gasped:

"Not yet, Tolas! Not yet!"

He could feel the men struggling with him start in surprise at his use of that secret name, and one muttered:

"He knows us!"

"But the pig will not know us long!" hissed another. "Quick—the knife! Let him have it between the ribs!"

It was so dark that Nat could not see more than two dim forms struggling with him, but he thought he recognized the two as Ramon and a companion, though who Ramon might be he could only guess.

Suddenly one of the men released his hold of the detective and drew back a little. The inference was obvious. He was getting out his knife.

"Not yet, Tolas! Not yet!" gasped Nat again, and, raising his right foot, he kicked out savagely at the dim form of the villain about to stab him. It was a trick Nat had learned from a Frenchman. With the heel of his shoe, the detective took the fellow amidships, or in the "breadbasket," if you prefer.

With a grunt that was half a groan, the scoundrel went down in a heap, though as he fell he hissed:

"Get him! He has disabled me! I have dropped my knife!"

There was ample evidence of this, for a tinkling sound followed Nat's lucky kick and the sleuth knew the dagger had fallen on the stones with which the alley was paved.

"The devil pig!" cried the other man, and Nat's eyes, now becoming accustomed to the gloom, made out the second assassin rushing at him. "This will be the end of him!"

But by this time the detective had his automatic out. He had no chance to take accurate aim, but he did not need to, for he could fire from the hip. And this he did—two shots in quick succession at the black mass of the man rushing at him.

There was a cry of pain and the fellow quickly wheeled about, changing his direction so that he was headed out of the alley.

"He is too much for us! Come—pronto!" he called to the other.

By this time the man Nat had kicked down was able to rise, though he was doubled up in pain. Thus the two fled, leaving Nat victor on the field and with spoils in the shape of a fine rope, made of braided horsehair, as he discovered later.

"Touch and go!" muttered the detective grimly as he straightened up. And then the street lamps suddenly shone again, though the alley remained shrouded in gloom. As Nat looked toward the entrance he saw, outlined against the background of light, a figure rushing toward him.

"Stand still!" the detective ordered. "I have you covered, and if you come a step nearer—"

"I'm a police officer!" came the sharp answer. "If you shoot—"

"Oh, all right! I beg your pardon," said Nat quickly. Though he determined not to be taken off his guard, and held his gun in readiness.

A moment later he saw a flashlight gleaming, the beams reflecting from the brass buttons of a member of New York's crack uniformed force. Then Nat knew he was safe and advanced, revealing his identity.

The policeman was a stranger to Nat Ridley, though the latter was evidently known, by reputation at least, to the patrolman, for the latter respectfully asked:

"Are you hurt, Mr. Ridley? Can I do anything to help?"

"No, they didn't get me," was the answer, "though it was a close call. They lassoed me as I passed the alley and dragged me in. What was the matter with the lights?"

"A fuse blew out at the power house, I guess. It's all right now. But who were they?"

"Oh, a couple of hold-up men," said Nat, not wanting to go into particulars.

"Well, I'd like to pinch them," said the officer. But when he and Nat had looked around the alley no trace of the assassins was found. The assassins had recovered and taken away the dagger. Only the rope remained, and Nat took charge of that. He thought he might find a use for it if he went on to Mexico.

By this time a crowd had gathered, attracted by the shots, as the officer had been, but it soon dispersed when Nat remarked to several who inquired:

"Oh, it was just a couple of bootleggers."

And so common has this form of industry become that it no longer attracts attention in the larger cities.

"Sure you aren't hurt?" asked the officer when Nat came out of the alley into the now brilliantly lighted street.

"Not at all. I kicked one man out and I think I hit the other with one of my shots. But evidently neither was much disabled, for they ran out just before you came up."

"I got here as fast as I could after I heard the shooting," apologized the patrolman. "But I was away at the other end of the block, and—"

"That's all right," Nat said. "No harm done. I was looking for another man and they happened to spot my pin, I suppose," and he motioned to a diamond he was wearing in his tie. "They wouldn't have made much if they got it, though," and Nat laughed, for the "diamond" was a paste one, a part of his disguise.

Nat went on his way, but the patrolman, jealous for the good reputation of his post, made a further search for the mysterious men, though he found no trace of them.

Nat Ridley did not mention his real suspicions concerning the two.

"I'll keep them guessing!" decided the sleuth. "If they look in the morning papers to see an account of this, they won't get much from the news."

Though he thus made light of one phase of the affair, there was another that worried Nat Ridley, and this was the closeness with which the Tolas were hanging on his trail.

"They have evidently sworn vengeance against all who have anything to do with the Lembergs or the oil wells," reasoned Nat. "I've got to watch my step. They must have shadowed me from my office. Well, I'll just stay away from there for a time—at least, I'll fool them."

He decided not to go to his apartment or to the office, and to carry out a plan he hastily made he went to the Herald Square Hotel, where he engaged a room. There, after a bath, a meal, and one of his big, black cigars, he telephoned a cipher message to Berry Todd at the latter's home.

"Come down here, Berry," requested Nat, "and bring number fourteen with you."

This was the number of a certain valise containing several disguises, and a little later the assistant detective arrived at the hotel with it. Berry himself was disguised as a country lawyer in New York for a holiday.

"Anything up, Chief?" he whispered to Nat when in the latter's room.

"Good and plenty!" was the answer. "I think I'm up against one of the slickest and most desperate gangs I've ever dealt with. You've got to help me, Berry."

"Surest thing you know, Chief. How?"

"You're going to be me."

"Going to be you?"

"Yes. I want you to make up to look like Nat Ridley, and, as me, leave the office openly to-morrow. Do it as publicly as you can—I mean speak to the elevator boys, the paper boys, greet anyone you see whom you know and get them to call you by name—I mean my name. In short, you and I are going to change identities."

"Suits me, Chief!" declared Berry.

"But you've got to be careful!" warned Nat.

"Careful of what—of making a break?"

"No. Careful not to get shot or stabbed or lassoed into a dark alley!" and Nat's voice was quietly warning. "Berry, we're up against a desperate game. It's asking you to take your life in your hands to impersonate me for a while. Are you game to do it?"

Without a moment's hesitation Berry answered:

"I sure am, Chief! Here's where I double for Nat Ridley!"

CHAPTER VII

LIGHTS OUT

Berry Todd and Nat made careful plans for what might happen during the next few days. It might be necessary for the assistant to continue the rôle of chief sleuth for some time, or until the Tolas were thrown off their guard.

"They were evidently out to do you," declared Berry, when Nat had told of the episode in the dark alley.

"They were," agreed the chief. "Though how they made their plans so quickly and got on my trail so easily I don't quite see."

"They're desperate!" decided Berry.

"Oh, yes. But worse, they have underground ways and means of getting information," added Nat. "Evidently the whole band is sworn to exterminate any who have a hand in keeping the oil wells away from them."

"Is Mrs. Lemberg willing to let the property go back to the original owners?" asked Berry.

"No, she isn't. She says part of it is hers by right now, since her husband is dead, and she will need the income from it to support her, since his business will not be carried on. She has the usual German thoroughness and determination to hold on, and I don't know that I blame her. But I'm working not so much to make secure the possession of the oil wells as I am to avenge Dan Steele, and also Lemberg. Though I was not friendly with the German detective, yet he belonged to the same national society as I do and we are sworn to protect each other. So it is war to the knife now between me and the Tolas."

"I'll help carry it on!" promised Berry.

A little later that night, having left certain disguises with Nat Ridley, the helper went back home and the following morning he appeared at the office in the semblance of Nat Ridley. So well did Berry simulate the dress and bearing of his chief that for a moment even Toodles was deceived, exclaiming as Berry entered:

"Good morning, Chief! You're a bit early."

"The early bird catches the worm, Toodles!" chuckled Berry. And there was something in the laugh that made the office boy look a second time, after which his eyes opened wide and he cried:

"Sweet daddy! If it isn't Berry!"

"Not so loud, young man!" warned the detective. "We don't want this little masquerade known!"

Toodles subsided, but Berry was pleased that he had made such good work of his disguise.

Nat passed a restful night in the Herald Square Hotel—that is, as much of the night as was left after his adventures, and in the morning went to his office, though not in his own character. He had made up to resemble a small town business man in New York to buy goods for the fall trade, which fact he spoke of as he ascended in the elevator.

Nat was so well made up that the elevator boys, who were well acquainted with him in his usual manner of appearing, thought him a stranger, and one of them directed Nat to the office of a commission merchant in the suite adjoining the detective's offices.

To throw off any spies who might be watching, Nat entered this office, but when the corridor was clear he came out, apologizing for having made a mistake, and entered his own rooms, where he found Berry, as Nat Ridley, waiting for him.

There was a hurried conference, and then the plan by which it was hoped to trap the murderers, or at least to get on their trail, was put into operation.

Berry, pretending to be Nat, left the office openly, and Toodles, following instructions, asked loudly as Berry held open the door leading into the corridor:

"What time will you be back, Mr. Ridley?"

"Can't say, Toodles!" was the equally loud answer. "If anybody asks for Nat Ridley say he's gone fishing," and with a smile Berry, as Nat, lighted one of the latter's black cigars, though the brand was a much stronger one than Berry liked to indulge in. But he had to do this to make the part perfect.

Watching his assistant from the partly opened door, Nat, who was still attired as a business man, saw Berry enter the elevator, greeting the boys who called him by name.

"Everything is working fine!" decided the detective.

As he watched he saw, coming from a washroom along the corridor, a small, dark man who glided like a snake into the elevator behind Berry. He had timed his entrance well, in order to be the last in the descending cage.

"There goes number one!" thought Nat, as he made ready to take the next down car. He had told Berry to wait in the corridor of the building before going out, and when Nat reached the street floor he saw his helper, who, of course, he pretended not to notice, start off down the street.

Behind him went the man who had glided out of the washroom.

"The chase is on!" grimly reflected Nat Ridley.

Then began what was like a desperate game of hide and seek. All that day Berry, as Nat Ridley, went about New York, into this office and that, where he was known, but where his disguise was not penetrated. And behind his assistant went Nat Ridley, now in one disguise and now in another, for he deemed it wise to change several times.

And between Nat and Berry was the small, dark man who was a clever shadower. That, the chief detective was forced to admit, for not once did he betray himself, and to anyone less sharp than Nat Ridley and Berry Todd, it would not have been known that any shadowing was going on.

It was not until late in the evening that Number One, as Nat had called him, was joined by another. This second man walked with a slight limp and as if he were in pain.

"I wonder if that's the fellow I shot or the one I kicked?" mused Nat as he noticed the halting gait. "It doesn't much matter, but it proves that I'm on the right track. Now I hope Berry remembers what I told him."

The assistant detective did, for he soon called a cab and, rather ostentatiously, asked to be driven to the Club Tamalle where Nat had seen the three men of the day before go in—the three, one of whom had ordered Ramon to keep watch over some "pig."

Nat, meanwhile, had made some inquiries and had learned that the club was the rendezvous of sportily inclined Mexicans, Spaniards and West Indians.

"I wonder how Berry, as me, will fare in there?" mused Nat, as he took another cab to follow his helper. "He'll be a bit conspicuous, I'm afraid, but it has to be done. After all, it isn't a private club, and anyone has a right there."

In the taxicab Nat Ridley made a final change in his costume, for he knew he was following clever and dangerous criminals and he thought one of them might have seen him some time during the day. Consequently, when Nat alighted at the Club Tamalle and paused to pay for his ride, he surprised a look of astonishment on the face of his driver.

"What game is this?" asked the man. "I didn't pick you up!"

"No," admitted Nat, with a smile, as he held up a couple of dollars extra to signal to the man to keep quiet. "But you're letting me down and you're getting paid for it."

"I'm wise," was the comment, and the cab rolled away while Nat, who was looking like a man out for a good time, followed Berry into the club where, it was rumored, high-priced and high-powered drinks could be had. Before entering, Nat had observed the two foreigners, one of whom walked with a limp, entering after Berry, who was still Nat Ridley, in disguise at least.

It did not suit the chief detective's plans to be too conspicuous in this well-known night club, so he tipped the head waiter to show him to a table rather screened from view, yet from which Nat had a good place from which to observe all that went on. There were a number of little private booths down one side of the room, and Nat was near one of these.

Not far away Berry had a table. Following instructions, Berry had picked up a woman, one of several who frequented the club for the purpose of having drinks bought for them, on which they reaped a percentage of the profits.

Berry began to act the part of a man out for an evening of pleasure. He ordered champagne, or what passed for such, and at the order his companion's eyes sparkled, for she saw her evening earnings greatly swelled.

While Nat was watching and pretending to drink some wine he ordered (and it was only pretending, for he was a teetotaler) the detective heard voices in the booth next to him.

"And from there we went to Paloma," a man said in low tones.

"Was there anything doing there?"

"Not much. We left, pronto, and headed for Rola—"

The remainder of the name was lost in the blare of the jazz band which struck up just then, but Nat thought he could guess what the rest of the name was.

"Rolamotaza—the place of the oil wells," thought the sleuth to himself. "We are coming on!"

The night club was now filling up rapidly, and Nat noticed that Berry was entering fully into the spirit of the occasion, with his pretty woman companion to aid him. Nat also noticed that the two men who had been shadowing Berry had been joined by a third who, in spite of a change in his clothes, was recognized as one of the trio who had passed Nat when he was examining the cab in which Lemberg had been murdered.

Nat saw these three change their table so that now they were next to the one where Berry sat, and the sleuth was wondering what that meant when he saw Berry give him a secret sign.

Nat had instructed his helper that if during the evening need arose to speak to his chief, a sign should be given, and Berry would go to the washroom, whither Nat would follow. There they could communicate with each other.

Accordingly, Nat rose slowly, as if without any definite object, and made his way to the washroom, whither he saw Berry bending his steps. The two entered, Nat behind Berry, and throwing a glance back over his shoulder, Nat observed the three Mexicans following. They, too, were headed for the private room.

"There's going to be something doing in about a minute, Berry," said Nat in a low voice as the two entered the room, followed a moment later by the three.

And something happened in less than a minute.

For the man who limped suddenly but purposely collided with Berry and at once cried in angry tones:

"What do you mean—pushing me? Beast! Pig! You have lamed me! Not for nothing shall a Gringo step on Don Castro!"

Like a flash the man drew a knife, but as he lunged for Berry his chief leaped forward and, with a skillful blow, sent the steel clashing to the floor.

At the same moment one of the other three shouted:

"Lights out!"

In an instant the place was plunged into darkness.

CHAPTER VIII

HALF A COAT

Silence followed the dramatic plunging of the rooms of the Club Tamalle into darkness, but the silence did not last long. And as soon as Nat Ridley had knocked aside the knife intended for his helper, the great detective got ready for action.

"They're after me!" grimly decided Nat. "Or at least after Berry, whom they have taken for me. There's likely to be a row!"

It came fully as soon as Nat expected, for he felt a rush of bodies about him, muttered imprecations in Spanish, and then he heard Berry's voice at his ear, whispering:

"Are you all right?"

"So far," Nat answered. "But I don't know how long I'll remain so. Did anything happen?" he went on as the two made their way in the darkness out of the washroom into the main apartment of the Club.

"Not yet. But I'm on the track of some of these fellows, and I think they got wise to me—thinking I was you."

"So far our plan works," murmured Nat. "But I'm wondering if they have spotted me as well."

There was no way of telling this at present. In fact, there was no way of determining anything in the darkness and excitement, for excitement there was in plenty.

"What is it?" some cried in English but with a Spanish accent. It was a woman's voice. There were a number of them in the club, some very handsome in a dark, Spanish way.

"It is the police!" came an answering feminine voice.

"Oh! Oh! A prohibition raid!" exclaimed several. "How silly!"

"Be careful!" warned the deep voice of a man, and Nat, hearing it, tried to recall whether it was that of Ramon or any of his associates. "It is no dry raid! There are spies and traitors among us! Be careful, my friends!"

"He's one of the fellows we want!" whispered Nat to his helper. "See if you can work yourself around to that side of the room. But be careful. You have your gun, of course?"

"Yes," answered Berry in low tones. "But I fancy these fellows would rather fight with a knife than a gun. I've got a knife, too."

39

"Watch yourself," warned Nat. "But get that fellow if you can."

"I will!" promised Berry, and he slid away.

Nat had backed to a wall, for he felt it safer in case of a fight which he thought would follow to have all his enemies in front of him.

The detective dimly saw forms swirling this way and that in front of him. Then, suddenly, he felt a pricking sensation on his left hand and he drew it quickly away with the thought that someone was trying to disable him by a scratch from the doped point of the miniature double dagger.

At the same moment Nat reached out with his hand and caught hold of a figure passing in front of him. He was surprised when a woman's voice screamed and she exclaimed:

"Oh, let me go! I have done nothing!"

"You tried to stab me!" hissed Nat in her ear. He realized that these Mexican murderers might have hired a woman to do some of their work.

"I stab you, señor? Never! I am but trying to get away. Are you Jules?" she whispered leaning so close to Nat that he could smell the perfume in her hair. "Oh, Jules, take me—"

"I am not Jules!" declared Nat. "But I felt a prick on my hand, and—"

"Pardon, señor, it was but a pin in my dress! Oh, why did I ever come here! Are you of the police?"

"No," answered Nat, which was the truth. "You have nothing to fear. There is a door—go!"

At that instant someone had opened a door leading into a corridor at the end of which a light burned dimly, and the illumination was sufficient to enable the detective to see a little.

Nat gave the unknown woman a shove toward the way of escape, since he decided she had had nothing to do with the case on which he was working. And the detective felt a distinct sense of relief when he heard the news about the pin. Imagination can play uncanny tricks at times.

Now several others, seeing the corridor door open, made a rush for the exit, so that it became jammed and there were grunts and imprecations from the men seeking to escape and screams and imploring calls from the women and girls.

Most of the habitués of the club, Nat realized, had nothing in common with the men he was seeking as the murderers of the Lembergs and Dan Steele. But the detective felt that some of the criminals, or at least their confederates, were present, and feared capture. Otherwise, the order of lights out never would have been given.

As Nat was wondering what was happening to Berry, the detective felt a man bump into him on the right side, and, at the same moment, one came at him from the left. The distant light in the corridor had gone out, and the place was once more in darkness, with a milling, pushing, jostling and excited crowd doing all it could to get away from the danger of arrest.

"Who are you?" asked Nat of the man on his left. "I am a stranger in New York. I came in here by chance and—"

He heard a whisper of Spanish words and though he did not sense all the meaning he had a feeling that the man on his left had called an order to the one on his right.

"They mean to do for me!" thought Nat to himself.

As quickly as a shadow moves, he dropped to the floor. It was not a moment too soon, for in the glow of an electric flashlight which someone switched on, Nat caught the gleam of a knife blade, and it was in the hand of the man who had been on his right.

The hand holding the knife lunged out, but the blade, instead of being sheathed in Nat Ridley's body, found a place in the companion of the Mexican. There was a cry of pain and a voice asked:

"Did I get the pig?"

"No, devil, you got me!" snarled another voice. "He has escaped us. I bleed! Get a doctor!"

"I'm glad he's bleeding instead of me!" mused Nat as he crawled on his hands and knees out of the danger zone. "That was a close one!"

If possible the excitement now became greater, for several had heard what the stabbed man, injured by his own friend, had said, and there was fear of more mistakes.

"Turn on the lights! Let us have light!" several implored.

"No! No!" came the answering replies. "There are traitors among us! They must be killed!"

"I wonder what's happening to Berry all this while," mused Nat. "I hope they haven't stuck a knife into him, thinking it's me. This case is developing faster than I thought it would."

He was reassured a moment later when, crawling into a corner, at that moment somewhat deserted, he felt another man crawling even as he was doing and a voice called into his ear:

"It's all right, Chief. I got some dope."

"You don't mean dope from the double dagger, do you?" asked Nat, for he recognized Berry's voice, though he could not see his face.

"No, I mean information. I got next to the fellow they call Ramon, and I heard him say the next meeting would be in Rolamotaza, a week from tonight. He mentioned a fellow named Don Castro."

"That's the chap who whipped out the knife in the washroom," remarked Nat. "So the scene is going to shift, is it? Well, I'll be on the job. I think we'd better be leaving here, Berry. We can't do much in the dark, and as soon as the lights go up the ones we want will have vanished. There's too much risk getting a knife in the back in the dark to stay here."

"Just what I was thinking, Chief. It's too bad they spotted us so quickly."

"Yes. They're slicker than most. Do you happen to know where the exit is, or any way of getting out?"

"I've got it spotted," was Berry's whispered answer. "Follow me, but keep low. There are too many of these birds lunging about in the gloom with their toad-stickers."

"So I found out. But someone else got the steel intended for me. It's best to be cautious," agreed Nat.

The two detectives started crawling on their hands and knees toward a place Berry thought would take them out of the dangerous place. And as Berry, followed by Nat, made his made way across the room, working in and out of a tangle of legs, the heavy body of a man suddenly leaped upon Nat Ridley's back. It was as if the detective had been tackled in a football game after dropping on the pigskin.

He grunted from the impact of the blow, but at once squirmed to get out from beneath the body. At the same time he began to reach out in the dark to grab any possible hand that might be holding a knife. Nat quickly succeeded in getting hold of a man's wrist.

"Give up!" commanded the sleuth. "I have you!"

With a quick twist and turn of a wrestling trick, he managed to get to his feet, pulling his assailant up with him. Nat reached out to grab the fellow's other hand, but the Mexican gave a squirm like an eel. There was a ripping, tearing sound, and Nat felt all resistance cease.

"What the deuce happened?" he asked himself.

Nat felt he had a garment in his hand—a coat he judged it to be, but whose or what it contained he could not tell.

"Six and a half! Six and a half!" Nat softly called.

This was a code number, indicating Berry's name. If the other detective was near he would answer.

"Seven!" was the reply in a whisper into Nat's left ear.

"What's wrong, seven?" asked Berry.

"All right now," Nat answered. "They had me down, but I got a coat off of someone."

"A coat?" questioned Berry.

At that instant the lights went up again, and Nat looked at what was in his hand.

"No, half a coat," he corrected, with a grim chuckle, for the garment was neatly ripped down the middle seam. "I got only half his coat, Berry."

"You're lucky to have that much," answered the other sleuth. "But look out. Here comes one of them with a knife!"

He and Nat looked up and across the room, from which a number of men and women with much disheveled clothing were now fleeing, since they could see the exits. And headed toward Nat and Berry was one of the three Mexicans who had started the trouble in the washroom. The fellow carried a wicked looking knife.

"This way!" Berry called to Nat, pulling him through a door and closing it after them. "This way out. And keep the coat."

"Half a coat is better than none!" chuckled Nat, as a heavy body crashed against the door, the key of which Berry quickly turned.

"Come on!" he called to his chief. "They're still after us!" And the two ran through a deserted room and out into a yard back of the Club Tamalle.

CHAPTER IX

THE WINDOW CLEANER

Most of the excitement in the Spanish club seemed to center around the front entrance, probably because, when the lights were dimmed, patrons who had nothing to do with the affair which brought Nat Ridley there, ran out that way.

A crowd gathered from the street, attracted by the shouts of the men and the screams of the women, and several police officers were on hand. Nat and Berry sensed this as they emerged from a rear door into the small yard, the chief detective still carrying the half of the coat which he hastily stuffed beneath his own garment, so it would not attract attention, for Nat was rather sprucily attired and to see a gentleman of his calibre carrying a torn coat did not argue well.

"Is there a way out of here?" asked Nat of Berry as, under the gleam of the moon, they looked about the yard which was not only surrounded by a high fence, but had buildings on both sides and at the rear.

"Surely there is!" declared Berry, who looked enough like Nat in that sleuth's regulation guise to be the latter's twin brother. "Like yourself, Chief, I never go into a place that I don't make sure there is a way out, and I spotted this one soon after I parked here this evening. Come along before that fellow takes the door off its hinges."

Indeed, it seemed that this might happen, for the man with the knife on the other side of the door was banging and kicking at it with enough energy to indicate that some of the panels would soon give way.

"He wants us bad!" chuckled Nat.

"They're all bad actors," agreed Berry. "My, but things happened quick after that fellow bumped into me! Only for you, Chief, I'd have a knife in my ribs now."

"Oh, I guess you could have taken care of him, Berry."

"Well, I'm just as glad you did it, Chief. Now here we go."

Berry ran to a certain part of the fence where, to the casual observer, there was no sign of a gate. But one was there, just the same, cleverly concealed, and a moment later it was open and the two sleuths saw before them an alleyway leading to the street.

Not much too soon, if they wished to avoid a fight, had Berry found the exit. For as he and Nat slipped through the secret gate, the door Berry had locked was burst open and the raging Mexican came rushing out, crying something in Spanish and brandishing his knife.

"Silencio!" someone uttered in sharp tones and there followed some commands in Spanish, hearing which the fellow who was eager to sheath his knife in Nat's ribs reluctantly turned back.

"Guess his boss got after him," chuckled Berry. "They don't want too much of a row here."

"There's been plenty of that," agreed Nat. "Well, I guess we can't get any more information here in these rigs, Berry. They're on to us. But you keep on being Nat Ridley and I'll change into something else to-morrow. I want to get a chance to look at this coat."

"Half a coat you mean," corrected his helper. "It should be easy to spot the man who lost it."

"Not likely he'd go about wearing part of a garment," objected Nat. "He'd either borrow one, or else go around in his shirt sleeves. No, let's beat it."

And beat it the two did, along a quiet back street and into a taxicab which took them to their offices. Nat allowed his assistant, who still impersonated him, to go in first, in case any of the Tola gang might be watching. The great detective himself made use of the freight elevator to reach his floor and, a little later, with the windows carefully shaded, he was examining the half a coat he had torn off the man who tried to kill him.

It was a cheap and ordinary garment, the kind of clothing sold in department stores, and probably would, in itself, afford no clew to the owner.

"But there may be something in the pockets," suggested Berry.

"Just what I'm going to find out," decided Nat.

From the outside pocket of the right side of the garment, which was the part the sleuth had, were taken some strong cigarettes so much indulged in by Mexicans and South Americans. There was also a clip of paper matches. These Nat put aside for future examination, though they were not very promising.

The inside pocket was richer in material to work on, for Nat brought out two rather worn letters in their original envelopes. They bore Mexican stamps and postmarks, showing they had been mailed in Rolamotaza.

"See if you can make out the dates on those postmarks, Berry," suggested Nat, handing the envelopes over to his assistant. "You'll find a magnifying glass in the second drawer of my desk on the right."

While Berry was at this task, Nat began a perusal of the letters themselves. They were addressed to Juan Castro, and the detective felt sure this was the man who wanted to knife Berry and also who had tried to attack him.

Written in Spanish as they were, Nat could make out only a few words here and there, for his knowledge of Spanish was small. He knew the Spanish word for oil, and he saw that scattered throughout the missive. He also saw the name Cora Ardell.

"That doesn't sound like a Spanish name," mused Nat, uttering it over and over again. "I wonder where she comes in? Well, I'll have to get these letters translated."

He glanced at the signatures. They were both the same, a scrawl which, as nearly as the detective could make out, resolved itself into the name Martolo.

"Another chap to look up!" mused the detective, through a haze of smoke from one of his strong, black cigars. "Well, any luck, Berry?" he asked his helper, who was puzzling over the envelopes.

"No, the postmark is so blurred I can't make any date on it. We might try photographing it—that sometimes brings out things you can't see with a glass."

"I don't know that it's important," Nat said. "I'll wait until I have these letters translated. The date may not matter. We'll call it a night, Berry, and quit. Now you go up to my apartment and get a good sleep."

"Your apartment!" exclaimed Berry. "What's the matter with my own home?"

"You forget that you are Nat Ridley," said the detective, with a chuckle. "Got to carry out the deception, Berry. Go ahead up. I've told Julian to expect you." Nat referred to his colored servant who looked after the Central Park West apartment.

"Oh, all right. I'll be living like a swell!" laughed Berry.

Nat, making some slight changes in his disguise, waited until his helper had gone. Then, putting the two letters carefully in an inner pocket, he left his office to go to the Herald Square Hotel again.

Forgetting none of the caution that was second nature with him, Nat Ridley looked about before stepping into the street. It was about one o'clock in the morning, but that, in New York, is only the "shank of the evening," and the streets in the vicinity of Times Square were filled with throngs.

Nat fancied he saw a man slink out of a doorway and start to follow him as the detective started down the street, and, chuckling to himself, Nat resolved to lead the shadow a merry chase. But the fellow, after following Nat a short distance, appeared to be satisfied that his quarry was not the man he wanted and turned back.

"He doesn't know me in this rig," Nat decided. "Well, adios, my friend. Adios," and with this Spanish farewell Nat went to his hotel and to bed.

He was at his office early the next morning, and one of the first things he did was to call for a Spanish interpreter whom he had come to the office to look over the letters.

"Write me out copies of these," directed Nat, giving the man a desk, pen and paper in a room off his own private office.

Several other matters claimed the detective's attention for the next fifteen minutes. But he finally disposed of the affairs, sending Baldy Stoler out on one case and Mary Dotley on another. Berry, as Nat, was ostentatiously busy writing in the front office, to throw off the track any of the Tola gang who might enter to spy out the situation.

As Nat was passing the desk of Toodles, the office boy, a shadow darkened one of the windows—the shadow of a man on the outside ledge.

"Who's that?" exclaimed Nat quickly.

"One of the window cleaners," Toodles answered. "The janitor sent word up early this morning that they'd be along our side of the building to-day."

"Oh, the window cleaner," murmured Nat, and he saw that that was the person whose shadow he had seen. The man, with his pail and chamois skin, was fastening his safety belt into the rings on either side of the casement.

Nat's stenographer spoke to him, asking him about a letter she was writing for him, and when he had set her right the sleuth turned back into his own private room, intending to ascertain how the translator was progressing.

As he put his hand on the knob there came from the room a cry of surprise, and, throwing open the door, Nat was in time to see the window cleaner leap in, knock aside the Spanish interpreter, grab something off the desk, and hurry out again.

"The letters! The letters!" cried the man Nat had hired. "The window cleaner took those two letters!"

CHAPTER X

OFF TO TEXAS

Like a flash and without stopping to ask questions, Nat Ridley leaped toward the window, through which, the Spanish translator indicated, the window cleaner had entered and left.

The man with the chamois was not in sight, but his pail was still on the broad, stone ledge, and Nat at once guessed what had happened.

"He walked along the coping here like a human fly and got into the next office," decided Nat. "He was a spy, disguised as a window cleaner! I thought he acted like an amateur when I first spotted him. The Tola gang is after me hot and heavy!"

Nat Ridley needed but a second to make up his mind.

"Where he went I can go!" exclaimed the sleuth. "Look after things sharp here for a minute or two," he called over his shoulder to Berry.

"Where are you going, Chief?"

"After that fellow!" exclaimed Nat.

"Be careful!" murmured the stenographer, who, with Toodles, had run into Nat's private office at the alarm given by the startled translator.

But Nat was already out on the ledge, which, aside from its height above the pavement, was a safe place to walk. In a few seconds the detective had entered the window adjoining his own—the window of an importing firm with the heads of which the sleuth had a slight acquaintance.

There was a clerk in the room into which Nat leaped from the window —a clerk who seemed rather startled.

"Another one!" he exclaimed, and Nat knew he had guessed right.

"Did a man just come in here?" asked the detective quickly.

"Yes. The window cleaner."

"He was no window cleaner," Nat stated, with a grim look. "But let that pass. Did he have anything in his hand?"

"Yes, some papers."

"Which way did he go?"

"Out through our office into the corridor. He said something about feeling sick and needing medicine. I thought you were another one when I saw you come in."

"You mean another window cleaner?" remarked Nat. "No, I'm not," and, as he was in disguise, the clerk did not recognize him. Nat let it go at that.

"Is anything wrong?" the young man asked, as Nat, after a look down the corridor and noting it was vacant, decided it would be useless to chase after the spy.

"No, not much wrong," was the reply. "I just wanted to ask him some questions. Another time will do."

Nat was anxious to get back and ascertain how much of the letters the translator had copied before they had been snatched away from him. So, with a nod to the clerk, Nat went back the way he had come, along the window ledge, somewhat to the surprise of the clerk.

The sleuth found his office force and the Spanish scholar awaiting his return somewhat anxiously.

"Did he beat it?" asked Berry.

"He sure did! It was quite a plan—pretending to be a window cleaner and even impersonating the janitor in telephoning up to tell Toodles he was coming. He got both letters, I suppose?" Nat ruefully asked the translator.

"Unfortunately of a truth, yes, señor," was the reply. "But not before I had made copies of them both. Here they are," and he held out two sheets of paper.

"Good!" cried Nat. "You copied them both, did you? Fine! As long as we know what the letters say we don't need the originals, unless they contain something incriminating."

"They do not seem to be of that nature," said the translator. "The missives do but contain some directions about oil wells and something of a contest over them. There are a number of names of persons and places."

"Good!" cried Nat again. "That is what we want."

Eagerly, he began perusing the translations of the letters found in the torn coat and, as he read, a pleased smile spread over the sleuth's face.

"This settles it!" murmured Nat.

"Settles what?" Berry wanted to know.

"About going to Texas and possibly to Mexico. I'll have to leave in a few days. I'm on the track of the double dagger gang now, all right!"

"Then you're going to run them down?" asked Berry.

"I am if it's humanly possible. I promised Mrs. Lemberg I would do what I could to avenge her husband's death. But I also have a big bone to pick with these devils in the matter of Dan Steele's death. Dan was once a pal of mine. I'll make those imps sorry they knifed him!" and Nat's eyes blazed.

Once more he read the translations, and then had his stenographer make copies of them which he put in his pocket, leaving the pen translations in his safe.

"That spy window cleaner wasn't as smart as he thought himself," chuckled Nat as he prepared to go out to arrange about transportation to Paloma. "He wasn't quite quick enough getting those letters back. You did your work quickly and well," he said to the Spaniard.

"I am glad that the señor is pleased," was the reply, and Nat added a generous bonus to the fee the man charged.

"Well, what's the game now?" asked Berry when he and his chief were alone in the private office after the excitement had calmed down. "Am I to go on being you?"

"Until you get orders to the contrary," Nat answered. "And now let me see—I've got to assume a new character. What would be a natural disguise for one who is going to the Mexican border? I think I'll go as a travelling hardware man, looking for orders for farm machinery—tractors and the like. I'll brush up a bit on the talk of the trade."

Nat Ridley had a wide acquaintance in New York, and among them was a friend in the whole-sale hardware business. Putting on a new disguise from his office stock—making up to look like an inconspicuous office clerk, Nat left his headquarters and sought out Jabez Norman, the big hardware man.

To the latter Nat explained enough of the matter to satisfy the natural curiosity of his friend, and then, for a day or so, Nat absorbed a lot of information about shovels, rakes, hoes, disk harrows, plows, tractors, and the like, together with trade and discount terms. He also managed to pick up a smattering of Spanish which was to stand him in good stead.

Having gotten enough hardware knowledge, he thought, to serve him in a pinch, Nat began to put his affairs in shape so that he could leave for his Mexican trip. For he did not doubt but that he would have to cross the border.

"These plotters and murderers probably slide back and forth over the line several times a week," the sleuth decided. "I must do the same."

The publicity following the murder of Lemberg, the solution of which baffled the police, and the stir made by the attack on Nat and Berry in the Spanish club, seemed to have sent the Tolas to cover.

During the time, after he had had the letters translated, when Nat was preparing to start for Paloma, there was no further attempt on the part of Ramon and his gang to interfere with the detective.

The unfortunate Lemberg was buried and Nat made a last call on his widow, promising to do what he could to bring the murderers to justice. Mrs. Lemberg was not able to give any more clews than those which she had already furnished the sleuth.

"My last word to you, though, Mr. Ridley," said Mrs. Lemberg as the detective was about to take his leave, "is to be on your guard."

"I will," he replied.

"You little know the desperate character of those men," she went on. "My husband did not realize it until too late, or he might be alive now."

"They certainly are desperate and cunning," agreed Nat, as he reflected on the fact that, in spite of all his precautions and disguises, the Tolas had, in some manner, found out about his visit to the Club Tamalle, learned that he had the letters, and had made such a successful attempt to get them back. It was only by chance that the translations had been made before the window cleaner played his trick.

"You shall hear from me," promised Nat as he bade Mrs. Lemberg a final good-bye.

"I hope in person," she answered, with a wan smile. And there was meaning and emphasis in what she said.

From her apartment Nat went to a railroad office where he bought a ticket and berth for Paloma. He thought he was well disguised and that he had come by such a roundabout route that none of the Mexican gang would be able to trail him.

Yet when Nat emerged from the office he was sure a dark, swarthy man, shabbily attired, who shuffled around the corner, was a spy watching him.

"I'll give him a run for his money!" decided the sleuth, with a grim look in his eyes.

Nat pretended to be in a great hurry and hastened along the street head down, looking at some papers he took from his pocket. But out of the corner of his eyes, he was watching the shabby man and saw him prepare to do some shadowing. Then, when opposite the fellow, Nat turned suddenly, as though to go back, having forgotten something. But he deliberately collided with the spy, and with such force as to knock him into the gutter where there was a puddle of water.

"Sorry!" exclaimed Nat. "You should look where you are going, my friend!" he added sharply.

For a moment the fellow said nothing, though his face grew darkly red with rage. Then he cried out a Spanish imprecation, shook his fist at Nat while scrambling out of the puddle, and added:

"Son of a pig!"

"Ah, ah! Señor Ramon or one of his friends! I thought so!" chuckled Nat, and before the fellow could arise to follow, Nat slipped into an office building, went up in the elevator, down again and out through another entrance, thus effectually throwing the shadower off the trail.

Yet with all his precautions and this strategic upsetting of one of his enemies, Nat Ridley felt that they were still on his trail, and he was more positive of it when he went to take the night train for Texas.

Some might ask why Nat did not arrest this rascal and force him to confess. The answer is, the great detective knew that this could not be done. The secret society was too powerful—no member would say a word, not even when in the shadow of death. If a man thought to squeal, he well knew that, once at liberty, his life would pay the penalty.

Tired out, Nat entered the sleeping car and was groping his way along the green-curtained aisle when the porter accosted him, asking the number of his berth.

"Twelve," answered Nat.

"Yais sah, dat's right! Lower twelve," and the colored bed-maker looked at Nat's ticket.

"Lower twelve and upper twelve," said Nat, holding out a second coupon.

"Upper twelve?" gasped the darkey. "Am dere two ob you?"

"No, I'm traveling alone," replied Nat, with a smile. "But I always buy two berths, an upper and a lower. I don't like anyone above me."

"Oh!" gasped the Porter. "Dat's too bad!"

"What's odd about that?" asked Nat. "It's a whim of mine."

"I wish I'd knowed dat, boss," the negro went on scratching his woolly head. "I didn't spect anybody had upper twelve, an' I jes' done put a gen'man in it."

"Oh, did you?" asked Nat sarcastically. "Well, then you can just rout the gentleman out and leave that berth empty. I've paid for two and I'm going to have them. No one sleeps above me!"

As he spoke the curtains of the upper berth parted and a dark face looked out.

"Pardon, señor," said a man in soft Spanish accents. "But there is no other place vacant in the train, and if you are not going to use this berth I shall be glad to pay you for your lower one and also for this."

"Nothing doing!" snapped Nat briskly. "That's my berth, and I'm going to have it."

An ugly look came over the face of the man in upper twelve.

CHAPTER XI

A FREE SPENDER

For perhaps ten seconds Nat Ridley stood in the aisle of the sleeper, looking at the man who confronted him from the upper berth. It was past midnight, and the passengers entering the train in the Pennsylvania Station went directly to bed or sat in the smoking compartment until ready to turn in, for the porter had all the sections made up.

Then the Mexican, Spaniard, or whatever he was, let his eyes fall before the steady gaze of the detective and thrust one leg out over the edge of the berth.

"I am sorry, señor," he began, but Nat was in no mood for polite rejoinder and merely remarked:

"It's all right—not your fault so much as it is this porter's," and he nodded toward the Negro. "But I always travel this way—can't sleep with anyone above me, and I'm not going to begin now. I guess you can find another berth."

"No, sah, boss—beggin' yo' pardon, we's full up!" exclaimed the porter. He saw that he had made a mistake and, looking to the tips in prospect—as well as to the bribe already pocketed—he tried to carry water on both shoulders and propitiate both travelers. "I's mighty sorry, boss," he went on to Nat, "dat I took one ob yo' two berths. I didn't s'pose any one man would want two, 'less he were twins. I figgered de clerk in de ticket office done make a mistake, an' so I told dis gen'men he could hab de upper."

"I'm sorry; but he can't," said Nat, with finality.

"I'll fix him up in de smokin' room," said the porter. "Come on, boss," he continued. "I kin fix you a good bed."

By this time the stranger was in the aisle, having climbed down the little ladder the porter brought for him. He had slipped a coat over his pajamas. He had evidently counted on a full night's sleep when Nat aroused him. The detective looked narrowly at the fellow, but his face was not familiar and Nat did not remember to have seen him before, either in the trio on the street near the cab containing the murdered body of Lemberg or in the Club Tamalle.

"But if he isn't one of the Tola gang, he belongs to the same race, and I don't trust them—not now," decided Nat. "I don't want them sleeping above me."

While the Mexican, with more murmured apologies, went to the other end of the sleeper, Nat piled his baggage into the upper berth and then sat down on the edge of the lower bed to think the matter out. Decidedly, he did not like what he had just discovered.

"I think they're on my trail, in spite of all my precautions," mused the sleuth. "They must have spotted me in the ticket office, and they easily found out where I was going and what berth I had. Then this fellow probably bribed the porter to let him come in here. Well, I've spiked their guns for a time."

But the more the detective thought it over the less he liked it, and he finally reached a decision that caused him to chuckle silently as he began to undress.

Before stretching out Nat rang for the porter and said:

"Don't worry, George, I won't hold it against you that you tried to get away with one of my berths. Here's a dollar, and when you get to the end of your run I may have another for you."

"Dat's de kind of talk I likes t' heah, boss!" and the porter grinned from ear to ear.

"But don't disturb me during the night, and make sure no one else does," warned Nat. "I've got a terrible temper when I'm awakened out of a sound sleep. See that I'm not disturbed."

"Dat's what I'll do, boss. I suah will!"

Then Nat went to sleep, first having taken the precaution of slipping his automatic under his pillow where it was ready to his hand. The train rumbled out beneath New York City, beneath the Hudson River, out over the Newark meadows and so toward the south and Texas. Nat Ridley slept, while, curled up none too comfortably on the leather seat in the smoking compartment was a dark-faced man whose scowl did not add to his looks. From time to time when alone he muttered something beneath his breath. But when the porter came in during the night, he always found his guest smiling.

Morning came, and, with the dollar bill in mind, the porter did not call Nat Ridley, whose temper was so short when suddenly aroused. Not until every other passenger in the sleeper was up and dressed did the porter venture carefully to open the green curtains of lower twelve to say softly:

"It will soon be brekfust time, sah!"

There was no answer, and the window curtains were still down, shrouding the berth in gloom.

"Does yo' still crave sleep?" asked the porter softly, as he reached forth a hand to shake, as he thought, the slumbering form. But his black fingers encountered nothing but bed clothing, and with an exclamation of surprise the porter swung back the curtains, letting in light enough to see that the berth was empty. The man who always traveled double had disappeared, bag and baggage.

"Well, whut yo' know 'bout dat?" gasped the black fellow.

"What is the matter?" asked the Mexican, pressing forward eagerly. "Has anything happened to the señor who was so selfish?" and from the cruel and crafty smile on the face of the man who had slept in the smoking compartment a close observer might have gathered that he would not greatly have minded had the "selfish" man died in his sleep.

"He's done gone—dat's whut happened!" exclaimed the porter. "An' he done owes me a dollar! De nex' time I lays myse'f out—"

But he checked himself suddenly and a grin replaced the scowl of his face as he reached down on the pillow and picked off a crisp dollar bill. Nat Ridley had not forgotten his promise.

"But where is the señor—what has become of him?" asked the Mexican.

"He mus' 'a' got off in de night," said the porter. "We made quite a stop at de junction, an' he mus' 'a' got off den. But he had a ticket clean through to Paloma," he added.

"Yes, I know he did!" exclaimed the Spaniard.

"Yo' knowed dat?" asked the porter suddenly.

"Well—er—I think I heard him say he was going there," was the confused answer. "Why should he get off short of his destination?"

"I dunno, 'less he couldn't sleep," chuckled the Negro. And then, as he kissed the dollar bill before putting it in his pocket, he added: "But I should worry! I got mine!"

* * * *

It was a hot night in Paloma, Texas, and the temperature of the night appeared to have imparted something of its nature to what was going on in the Cordova Club, a resort much frequented by Americans as well as by Mexicans filtering over the border line.

A jazz band was blaring out its most blaring music—a band composed, it would seem, of negroes, though in its advertisements the Cordova Club made much of its Spanish orchestra. There was a scurrying to and fro of waiters bearing tall glasses of cooling drinks, and it might be argued, other drinks, cooling in so far as ice was concerned, but which seemed composed of liquors that set the blood tingling.

In other words, it was pretty freely whispered about in Paloma that much stronger "stuff" than the legal half of one per cent. was freely dispensed at the Cordova Club.

It was what might be called a high class resort—that is, evening dress for the men and women predominated, though it was not absolutely required that a man have on his "soup and fish," or that women must be bared of arm and shoulder. But that was usual.

Among others who sauntered into the gay and blaring club this hot night was a well-dressed man who seemed bubbling over with good nature. His evening clothes were worn with an air as if he put them on each night to saunter forth for hours of gay life, and he had that about him which caused the head waiter to hurry forward deferentially to ask:

"How many, sir?"

"I'm alone," was the smiling answer. "And I'd appreciate it, captain, if you could put me at a table with some gentlemen where I can enjoy myself."

"Of a surety, señor," was the ready response. "I will place you among what we call the Bohemians."

"Fine and dandy! That suits me right down to the ground!"

A little later the well-dressed stranger was ushered into a circle of equally suitably attired men at a central table, near the dancing floor. As the head waiter left this stranger remarked:

"I suppose there will be no objection if I order some bubble water for the crowd?"

"Bubble water, señor?" questioned the waiter who had come up at a signal from the captain.

"Champagne!" exclaimed the stranger. "Gentlemen, allow me to introduce myself," he went on. "Bill Brice is my name. I'm traveling for the National Hardware Corporation and I'm taking a night off. Will you oblige me by imbibing a bit of bubble water with me?"

Would they? You should have seen their eyes sparkle at the mention of the sparkling wine. And the waiter, at a signal from his chief, hurried off to fill the order.

Champagne for the whole table! It was seldom done, but—

"He must be a free spender," one of the crowd remarked as they all gave their names to "Bill Brice" in return for his own. "Well, they can't come too free for me."

Then the jazz band blared on, the glasses tinkled, and the champagne frothed while, in a quiet corner, a dark-faced man remarked softly:

"So, he got here after all, did he? But when did he leave lower twelve and slip away from me? That is what I would like to know."

CHAPTER XII

EL CAPITAN

None of the parties in the Cordova Club was any more lively or gay than the one at the table where Bill Brice, of the National Hardware Corporation, sat buying champagne. There were songs in English and Spanish, though it must be admitted the Spanish ones were the best sung since, it developed, most of the men who were partaking of the hospitality of Bill Brice were Mexicans, though many claimed to be pure Castilians.

"This is the life for me!" boasted Mr. Brice, who still had in front of him the same first glass of champagne he had ordered at the start of the evening. He had taken a single sip, when his new friends insisted on drinking his health, but thereafter the bubbles rose from the bottom of his glass unnoticed.

One of the Mexicans, who had said he ran a moving picture theater in Paloma, noticed this and remarked on it.

"I had plenty before I drifted in here," explained Mr. Brice, "and I find it sets better on my stomach if I smoke a bit between drinks, my friend."

With that he pulled out a strong, black cigar and began puffing on it, blowing smoke rings to the no small admiration of his companions.

The evening wore on, the band played louder, more men and women entered the club, and the waiters hurried here and there with their bootleg products, for so near was the Mexican border that the customs officials were hard put to prevent contraband being smuggled over the line.

"This is the life!" exclaimed Mr. Brice more than once. "I'm about sick of the hardware line," he confided to his neighbor. "I wish there was some other way of making money. You wouldn't like to be selling tractors, plows, hoes and rakes all your life, would you?"

"Of a surety not, señor," was the reply.

"Maybe you make yours in some easier way?" suggested Mr. Brice. "Say oil wells, now."

"Let us say oil wells," agreed the other, with a smile.

"No, but seriously," went on the free spender, "are you in oil?"

"I am, of a surety, señor."

"And do you know where I could invest some money?"

The eyes of the other gleamed as he answered:

"Naturally. If you are interested—"

But he broke off as a commotion at the entrance indicated something unusual going on, and a moment later a party of several men and women, headed by an individual who would attract attention anywhere, entered the club. He was a big, handsome, swarthy man, and he wore a uniform that became him well.

"Is he the commander-in-chief of the Mexican army?" asked the man who had called himself Bill Brice.

"That is El Capitan," was the answer.

"Captain of what?"

"He was of the army," was the reply. "But he is retired. It was he of whom I was about to speak when you mentioned investing in oil, my friend. He has large holdings, señor. El Capitan would be the one for you to know."

"Then I'm going to cultivate his acquaintance," was the laughing comment. "And when Bill Brice goes cultivating, something grows," and he chuckled with easy good nature. "Could I meet this captain?"

"He is called El Capitan, señor," said the other, making three, full syllables of the name. "He is also Martolo."

"Martolo!" exclaimed Mr. Brice with such sudden energy that his companion stared at him in surprise and asked:

"You know him already, then, señor?"

"Oh, no—no," and the hardware man laughed and blew another ring of smoke. "But I have heard the name."

The distinguished former soldier and his party were deferentially escorted to a table, and at once ordered champagne, so it would seem that Mr. Brice had done the proper thing.

The evening wore on, the club becoming gayer and gayer, and the bottles of "bubble water," accumulating at the table of Mr. Bill Brice—but they were empty bottles. Meanwhile, he had talked further with Señor Valdez, his nearest neighbor, about investing in oil wells, and had received the promise of an introduction to El Capitan later in the evening.

As a matter of fact, there was none of the evening left. It was long past midnight, but still the jazz band played on and the glasses tinkled while the dancing became more and more abandoned.

"It is a good time now, I think," said Señor Valdez to the hardware man, "to have you meet El Capitan. He is in the mood."

"Suits me," was the answer. "I sure do want to get out of the game of selling plows and tractors. It isn't my line."

Mr. Bill Brice spoke truly, his line was detective work, and the free spender was none other than Nat Ridley. He had decided to take no chances in the sleeper and had slipped out at the junction, laying over until the next through train to Paloma, and, thereby, greatly surprising not only the porter, but the man who had unlawfully been in upper twelve.

Many of these who had been at the table of Mr. Brice, or Nat Ridley, had by this time drifted away. The gay party was breaking up, but there were still congenial spirits in the club, and the center of life was now about the table of El Capitan.

Thither Señor Valdez and Nat Ridley, known to the Mexican as "Bill Brice, a free spender," made their way, moving amid the dancers, the coming and going of guests and the rushing of eager waiters.

El Capitan Martolo seemed very popular indeed. Someone was continually leaning over his shoulder, whispering in his ear, or pledging his health in a glass of champagne. Now and then men who glided in to speak to him glided out again as quickly, bent on some mission, it would seem.

"El Capitan is a very busy man," commented Nat. "Very busy—with oil?"

"With oil—and other interests," admitted Señor Valdez, with a smile. "If it pleases him to take you into his confidence you will be a lucky man."

"I guess I'm pretty lucky, anyhow," returned Nat. "If I wasn't, I wouldn't be here."

"You were in some danger, then, Señor Brice?"

"Yes, you might call it that. But I'm generally able to take care of myself. I suppose there is trouble here now and then?" His voice was questioning.

"Trouble? Of what sort, señor?"

"Well, you know the prohibition authorities—"

"Oh, they are a joke!" laughed Señor Valdez. "We never have any trouble from them. But it is true that, now and then, someone drinks not wisely but too well, and there is what you call a fracas."

"Oh—a fracas," repeated Nat. "You mean shooting and all that?"

"Yes. It is well that the señor is lucky. But to-night is a quiet one. Nothing will happen."

Nat recalled that statement a little later and had to smile to himself as he did so, in spite of the seriousness of his situation.

He and his new friend were almost at the table of El Capitan when a man, who seemed greatly excited, brushed his way none too gently through the press of persons and handed the former officer of the Mexican army a letter. At once a wild desire to see that note took possession of Nat Ridley, and he made up his mind he would get it.

El Capitan read the missive through quickly—it was not long—and he was thrusting it into the side pocket of his coat, having directed the messenger with a nod to stand aside a moment, when Nat was brought up for introduction by his new friend.

"He would like to invest in oil wells," said Señor Valdez.

"Ah—oil wells? It takes much money," said El Capitan, with a smile, as he shook hands with Nat and the latter noted the powerful build of the Mexican.

"Well, I happen to be pretty well fixed," Nat, with an easy air, replied. "And I'm tired of selling hardware. So, if you could put me wise to something in the game—"

"Ah, yes, Señor Brice, it is a game!" declared the army man. "I have been in it some time, but there is yet much for me to learn. But I shall be glad to teach you."

"Thanks, El Capitan," responded Nat. "I can't learn any too soon if I want to make anything. There are a lot of wells being put down now, aren't they?"

"A few, Señor Brice, and I control some of them. Now, if you wish to talk business," and the Mexican's eyes gleamed, "I shall be happy to receive you at my office."

At that moment El Capitan struck a match to light one of his strong cigarettes, and Nat at once pulled out another strong, black cigar, bit off the end and leaned over, very close to the Mexican, to take advantage of the occasion, murmuring:

"A little of your fire, if you please, El Capitan?"

"As much as you please, señor," was the gracious response, and Nat's hand went in a stealthy fashion he had learned from an expert pickpocket to the side pocket of the Mexican. When the detective leaned up the letter the messenger had brought had been transferred from one pocket to the other.

There was further talk of oil wells, and Nat made a date with the big officer to talk more the following day, or rather, this same day, for it was now long past midnight.

Excusing himself for a moment, the detective went to a washroom, where he took out the letter he had purloined. He wanted to read it before anything could happen.

As he expected, when he unfolded it under the lights in the small anteroom, the missive proved to be in Spanish. But Nat had in the last week or so given himself enough mastery of the language to make out something of the contents of the note. He saw that it referred to the Lemberg family and to further plans for making them give up their title to the oil wells which were wanted to further the plans of the Tola gang.

"I'm on the right track!" mused Nat as he thrust the letter back in his pocket to return to El Capitan. As he left the washroom the detective noticed the messenger who had brought in the note coming out after him, but he thought little of it at the moment.

A little later Nat invited El Capitan to share a bottle of champagne with him, though the detective did not intend to drink any of the wine himself. It was while he was seated at the former officer's table that the messenger who had delivered the note approached. He made a sign to El Capitan and, at the same moment, spoke in Spanish. Nat looked up in time to see the messenger pointing what seemed to be an accusing finger at him.

El Capitan shot out a sharp question, and there was a quick interchange of excited words. Then El Capitan turned to Nat and began:

"It seems, señor, that you have—"

"The fat's in the fire!" was the thought that rushed into Nat Ridley's mind.

"Pardon," murmured a voice in Nat's ear. A hand touched his shoulder, and a man he had noticed drinking heavily at the captain's table confronted him. There was a Mexican girl, pretty in a bold sort of way, standing beside Nat's accoster, and the man went on: "This lady say you have insulted her!"

"I have insulted her?" cried Nat, taken, naturally, by surprise. "I never saw her before and haven't even spoken to her!"

"Nevertheless the señorita say you have given the insult," murmured the man, and there was a dangerous look in his eyes. "You must to me, her affianced, give satisfaction."

"Oh, so that's the game, is it?" cried Nat. "Well, I—"

At that moment a shot rang out from somewhere in the crowd back of the accuser. The first shot was followed by several others, and Nat dropped to the floor just as the lights began to go out.

A moment later the place was in darkness and there were confused shouts and cries of alarm.

"At their old tricks!" murmured the sleuth, as he began to crawl toward a flight of steps leading into the cellar from which the supply of wine was brought up and of which he had taken note earlier in the evening.

CHAPTER XIII

IN THE DUNGEON

Nat Ridley was doing some quick and hard thinking as he made his way like an eel along the floor toward the cellar stairs. He realized that he was in great danger, but he could not be certain that the shots fired had been aimed at him.

"If those shots weren't for me, there would have been some coming my way in a little while," mused the sleuth. "That messenger was sharper than I thought. He spotted me with El Capitan's letter," and Nat's hand went to his pocket to make sure he still had the note. He also wanted to be certain that he had his automatic.

"Tried to force a quarrel on me! That's what they did!" decided Nat as he hurried to the head of the stairs in the darkness. Fortunately he had noticed them well when the lights were on, as he had thought he might have to make use of them.

"I wish I knew more Spanish," mused Nat, who was by this time at the head of the cellar steps. "I'd like to know just what El Capitan said when he heard the messenger give me away. Well, I'll have to let that go and save myself. Whew, they're going it in there!"

Indeed, great excitement now prevailed in the main room of the night club. Several more shots were fired, but Nat knew now that the bullets could not reach him. He closed the door back of him and, not relishing going down unfamiliar stairs in the dark, he took out his flashlight.

This he screened by holding it in his hand so that only the faintest glimmer came from between his fingers. But it was enough to enable him to see so he would not stumble.

Nat expected to observe some of the club servants or habitués come running up the steps at any moment to ascertain what the excitement was about. But he saw no one, and the change from the noise of the main room to the comparative quiet of the cellar was a relief. Nat Ridley was not an admirer of jazz, and loved to be quiet.

He reached the bottom step and noted that the cellar was a large one, extending in two directions from the flight of stairs. There were dim lights burning here and there, and in the distance Nat could hear the tinkle of glasses and bottles.

"They must have private rooms down here, where they have all sorts of high jinks," reasoned the sleuth. "Well, I'll give it the once over."

There was now no need of using his flashlight, for the cellar had its own illumination, though not of the brightest, and Nat did not want to make himself a conspicuous object by holding the little electric torch in his hand.

He put it in his pocket and, making sure again that his automatic was in readiness, he stepped out and walked softly along the cement floor of the cellar.

"Guess I'll give that merry party the once over," decided the detective as the noise of laughter, singing, and the tinkle of glasses and bottles became more distinct. "I might pick up some information."

Keeping close to the wall and treading softly, at the same time casting a look behind him now and then to make sure he was not followed, Nat advanced toward that part of the cellar whence issued the noise of merrymaking.

It came from what seemed to be a wine vault, but in which a table was set with food, and about this were grouped a number of men and women who were evidently servants of the club.

At this hour of the morning their duties were pretty much over, and it was plain that they had gathered to enjoy, though in a more limited way, the same fun as that indulged in by the patrons upstairs.

"I don't believe I care to mingle with them," thought Nat. "It might arouse suspicion. But it's queer they don't go up to see what all that row is over their heads."

For the Cordova Club seemed undergoing a raid or something of that sort. Men and women were rushing about and occasionally a shot was fired. The band had stopped playing, and Nat could only account for the indifference of the servants on the assumption that they were used to all sorts of queer antics on the part of the jazz-mad patrons.

"They don't want to mix in it," reasoned Nat.

He turned aside from the room where the early morning meal was in progress, and started back the other way. As he turned a corner he collided, full tilt, with a man.

In an instant Nat had his automatic out and pressed it against the stranger's ribs, with a whispered order to keep silent. But in the light that filtered around the turn in the corridor, the sleuth saw that he had little to fear from the unknown.

He was an old man with white hair and a bent and stooped back—evidently an aged servant, perhaps the keeper of the hidden store of wine and liquor.

"Pardon, señor," said the old man in a low voice. "It was my fault—I did not see you coming."

"Nor I you," admitted Nat, glad that the fellow spoke English. Then with a happy thought the detective added: "El Capitan sent me—"

He let the sentence end there. It was better not to be too explicit. And, in a manner of speaking, El Capitan had sent Nat to the cellar. For had not the messenger made the disclosure, and had not the former army officer made so threatening a gesture, Nat would still be upstairs.

"Ah, El Capitan—yes, señor. He sends many down here. You are welcome."

Nat was wondering what the answer was to this when the old man whom the detective had released from the first grip he had taken on his arm, walked away, making a sign to Nat to follow.

"I wonder where he wants to take me?" mused the sleuth, and he was in half a mind to refuse to go. But then he wanted to get out of this cellar before those above discovered that he had come down, and he thought the old man might show him an exit.

But the man had something else in view, for, muttering to himself, he led the way until he stopped before a small room fitted with a small table and two chairs. The table was set for a meal, though there were no viands on it.

"Pleased to be seated, señor," invited the old man with a deferential bow. "I will order the food prepared. Doubtless the lady will be here soon?"

It was a question, and Nat could not conceal his surprise as he asked: "What lady?"

"Why, señor, the one you are to dine with."

"I haven't any appointment to dine here with a lady," said Nat, with a grim smile. "There must be some mistake."

"Pardon, señor, no mistake," murmured the old man. "El Capitan said he would send to me this evening an Americano who would dine in seclusion with a lady. I made ready this rendezvous, and you come. I but ask where the lady is."

"And I tell you—" began Nat, and then he held his tongue. He began to see it now. Doubtless the Mexican had plans concerning another American and things had gone wrong. The old servant had naturally supposed Nat was the one expected.

"Let it ride that way," decided the sleuth. "I may find out something this way. I'm taken for somebody else. Well, I'll play the game." Then to the old man he said: "The lady—she will be here soon. Get the food ready. And show me the way out—I mean how to emerge without the need of climbing the stairs."

"Of a surety, señor, yes, there is another way out. See, you have but to press here," and he indicated a certain stone in the cellar wall, leaning against it. At once what seemed to be a section of the foundation swung back and a short flight of steps was disclosed.

"So that's the way out?" asked Nat.

"That is the way out, after one has dined here with the lady," said the old man, smiling.

Nat watched him walk out and along the cellar, doubtless toward the kitchen, for the smell of cooking was plain to the nose of the sleuth. Nat looked about the room. Aside from the secret staircase, the opening to which had been closed, there was nothing about it different from other basement rooms, many of which are used in New York for night clubs.

"All the same I want to see if I can work that secret door," murmured Nat. He found, to his satisfaction, that the operation was simple once it was known what stone to press, and he opened and closed the stone door.

Then, desiring to make sure he was not being spied upon, the detective stepped outside the private room. He moved a little away from the entrance and as he did so he heard, near at hand, a girl's voice crying:

"Oh, don't! Don't strike me again! I can't stand it!"

The heavy tones of a negro woman snarled:

"I's done got to beat yo' ef yo' don't sign dem papers for de captain! Stand up now an' take yo' medicine!"

"No! No!" pleaded the other voice.

Nat Ridley leaped into action. The voices seemed to come from behind the cellar wall, but he flashed his light and saw a heavy wooden door in the wall near the door of the private room.

It was the work of but a moment for the detective to swing back the door, which was closed but not locked, and then he found himself looking into a veritable stone dungeon, in the middle of which knelt a beautiful, blonde girl.

Standing over her, with a blacksnake whip upraised, was a powerful negro wench.

"Don't! Don't beat me again!" pleaded the girl. But the lash fell with stinging force across her back.

CHAPTER XIV

THE BOMB

"Stop!" cried Nat Ridley in a ringing voice as he leaped forward and stood in the circle of light cast by an electric bulb suspended from the ceiling.

"Stop!" he cried again, and the Negress who had raised the lash let it fall as she turned in astonishment to look at the intruder. "Hit her again," hissed Nat in a low voice, "and I'll tie you up, you black wench, and cut you into ribbons with that same whip!" It was no time for polite talk, the sleuth reasoned.

"Oh, save me! Save me!" pleaded the girl, and she started to crawl toward Nat, for she had slumped over at the first blow.

"I'll save you all right!" returned Nat grimly, as he took out his automatic. "What is it all about, anyhow?"

"Oh, I don't know! I was kidnapped a few days ago and brought here to this terrible place! Some Mexicans visited me several times and wanted me to sign some papers. When I wouldn't they said they would make me. And this is the beginning of that, I suppose," the girl sobbed.

"What sort of papers did they want you to sign?" asked Nat, wondering if he was going to be involved in another mystery. The double dagger and the oil wells were enough for one man at a time, he thought.

"They were papers—" began the girl, when the Negress who had backed away at Nat's entrance seemed to recover her courage. She lurched forward and snarled:

"Keep yo' mouth shet, white girl, ef yo' wants to see daylight ag'in. Don't talk!"

"Don't mind her," advised Nat. "I am here to help you if I can."

His interference seemed to anger the Negress, for she took a step nearer her captive, again raising the lash as she exclaimed:

"White man, ef yo' knows whut's good fo' yo', beat it!"

Before the lash could fall Nat Ridley leaped at the hideous black creature and tore it from her grasp. He brought it down with stinging force across her shoulders, causing her to scream with pain and rage.

The next moment Nat had put his hand over her mouth, for he did not want her to give the alarm. With the other hand he caught up a rag he saw on the floor and in a trice had gagged the Negress.

"Oh, to think I am no longer in her power!" murmured the girl, who rose to her feet and sat down in one of the chairs. "Can you help me get out of here?"

"I'm going out myself," declared Nat, "and I'll take you with me. So that's your game, is it?" he exclaimed as, having gagged the black woman he leaped aside in time to escape a kick from one of her big feet clad in a heavy shoe. "Well, I know a trick worth two of yours."

A skillful motion of his foot and he had tripped the wench. She fell heavily and before she could roll over Nat had tied her hands and feet, with the long lash of the black snake whip. Then he rolled her into a corner and proceeded to take stock of the dungeon and the girl captive he had saved.

"How strong you are!" murmured the girl, clasping her hands. "I never thought I would be saved. You came in the nick of time."

"You have to—in this business!" returned Nat grimly. "Now then, if you can tell me something about yourself and why you were brought here," he went on, "I may be better able to help you. We can't stay here too long. I expect some of that crowd will be down before long, looking for me," and he pointed upward. The noise of the crowd in the Cordova Club was still audible, though, as yet, none of those from above seemed to have come down into the basement.

"My name is Cora Ardell," said the girl, who had recovered some of her composure. "I live in New York, but for the past six months I have been acting as a stenographer and typist for my cousin in Rolamotaza."

"In Mexico?" asked Nat, as he recognized the name of the town, and also recalled having seen the name Ardell in some of the Lemberg reports.

"Yes."

"What line of business is your cousin in?" asked Nat.

"He was in the oil business—he owned oil wells," replied Miss Ardell. "But he doesn't any more."

"Did he sell out?"

"He was killed," was the simple answer.

"Was your cousin's name Carl Lemberg?"

"Why, yes!" exclaimed the girl in surprise. "How did you know!"

"No matter—please answer my questions," said Nat.

"He is my cousin, surely," Miss Ardell answered. "But I didn't mean him when I said he was killed. I was speaking of his brother Henry. They are both my cousins, of course. But Carl wasn't killed."

"I am sorry to inform you that he was—a few days ago," said Nat gently.

"What, Carl killed too?" burst out Cora Ardell. "Oh, how terrible! How did it happen?"

"By the double dagger," whispered Nat, so the negress would not hear.

"The double—" began the girl.

"Hush!" cautioned the sleuth. "She may be listening. Yes, Carl Lemberg was murdered in New York by the double-dagger gang. They killed Henry, didn't they, and also August Lemberg?"

"They were both murdered. That is all I know," said the girl. "They had bought some oil wells in Mexico and, as I was out of a position in New York, they offered me a good one here. So I came on. Then everything seemed to happen at once. For several days I noticed that my cousin and his uncle were worried about certain letters they received. But the business went on and was paying well. They gave me some shares in the oil wells in addition to my salary.

"Then, suddenly, one day, Henry Lemberg was killed. He was found stabbed to death in a lonely place. The police said Mexican bandits had done it. I didn't know what to do. I was getting afraid. Then August was killed in much the same way."

"Did the Mexican police do anything?" asked Nat.

"They came and asked a lot of questions and went through a lot of motions," the girl replied, "but it didn't amount to anything. Then some of the young men clerks, who had also come from New York with me to work for my cousin, sent word to Carl in New York and he had a detective come down to try to catch the murderers. Well, the detective came, and—"

"His name was Dan Steele, wasn't it?" asked Nat softly.

"Yes. How did you know?" and Cora Ardell looked at her questioner with widely opened eyes.

"It is my business to know," remarked Nat. "And poor Steele was also murdered; wasn't he?"

"Yes! Oh, yes!" There was a tearful catch in her voice. "Oh, who are you, anyhow?" she asked, gazing searchingly at Nat. "How do you know all these things? Who are you and how did you come just in time to rescue me from that horrible Negress?"

"In answer to the first questions," Nat replied, still speaking almost in a whisper, "I will say that I happen to know about the killing of Dan Steele because he was my friend, and, just before his own murder, your cousin Carl engaged me to ferret out the men who had killed his uncle and his brother."

"Then you are a—" began the girl.

But Nat, motioning to the bound wench, made a sign of caution. But he saw that Cora had guessed his profession.

"Now tell me," went on Nat, "and I must know in order to decide in what way to act, how did you happen to come here?"

"I was kidnapped and brought here."

"By whom, how, and when?"

"I don't know by whom," the girl answered. "But it was about a week ago and this is how it happened."

"Tell me all the circumstances that occur to you," urged Nat. "A point that seems small to you may loom large to me. Omit nothing."

"There isn't really very much to tell," Cora said. "After Henry Lemberg was killed—murdered I suppose I should say—there was much confusion in the office. This was doubled when a few days later his uncle was stabbed to death. The whole office force was thrown into a state of terror, for we thought a race war had broken out.

"We didn't know how to attend to business, and there was much to be done, for the oil wells turned out to be more valuable than was at first supposed. You know my cousins had some wells of their own and also bought others in which certain Mexicans had interests. These last wells were not thought to be worth much, but after the Mexicans' interests had been purchased by my cousins and the Mexicans had left, these wells proved worth more than all the others put together."

"So I heard," remarked Nat.

"Well," resumed the girl, "you can imagine what a state the business was in after the two murders. Then Mr. Steele came down to help us straighten things out. But in a short time he was killed. Then terror seemed to take possession of all the young men clerks who had been brought from New York to help with the office business, and they packed up and went back to the United States."

"What did you do?" asked Nat.

"Why, I stayed on and did what I could to save my cousin's business!" exclaimed Cora, with spirit. "I wasn't afraid until—until—"

"Well, until what?" asked Nat, as she hesitated.

"Until one day I received a card on which was scrawled a warning to leave the country," said the girl in a whisper. "I was told that I would have a week, after that—"

"Well, after that?" encouraged Nat.

"There was no direct threat," said Cora. "In place of words was the picture of a double dagger."

"I thought so!" exclaimed Nat. "The sign of the Tola gang. I take it you didn't desert?" he asked.

"No. I telegraphed Carl in New York, asking what to do. I wanted to save the business if I could, for I had an interest in it, and I knew the families of the murdered men might be in want. The oil wells are very valuable."

"I believe so," agreed Nat.

"But before I could get word back from Carl," resumed Cora, "one night I was called to the door of my boarding place with a Mexican family. I was told someone wanted to see me. I thought it was a business message. But as soon as I went out of the house I was seized in the dark, a blanket was thrown over my head, I was put in an auto, and the next I knew I was brought here. Since then I have been kept a prisoner, and several times Mexicans whom I did not know have come here with papers they wanted me to sign."

"Which you didn't do?" asked Nat.

"No; and I never will! They put the Negress over me as a guard, and yesterday they gave me what they said was the last warning. It was to the effect that unless I signed the papers I would be lashed with the whip until I did. Just before you came one of the Mexicans was down here, and, when I refused, he told the woman to get the whip. I—I guess you saw the rest," and Cora finished with a little sob.

"I saw the rest!" declared Nat, with a grim look in his eyes. "And I'm going to have a hand in the rest. Now if you are able to come—"

He interrupted himself to listen. The noise upstairs seemed to have quieted down, but there were audible footsteps coming along the stone-paved floor of the cellar. Nat arose and drew his gun.

"What is it?" asked Cora in a whisper.

"I don't know," was his answer. "But it is best to be ready for them. Get behind me."

The girl moved into a position of safety just as a big husky Negro followed by two Mexicans entered the dungeon. They appeared surprised at what they saw—the wench bound in a corner and a calm white man guarding the girl prisoner.

"Who is yo'?" leered the colored man.

"What business is that of yours?" countered Nat Ridley.

"I'll soon show yo' what business I has, white man!" shouted the Negro. "Come on, boys!" he called to his Mexican companions.

Nat Ridley hastily made a plan. Reaching back, he took hold of Cora's hand and whispered from the corner of his mouth:

"Be ready to follow me! We're going out of here!"

The Negro man seemed to anticipate that something was coming, for he lurched forward, farther into the dungeon, and cried:

"Get around him, boys! Knife him ef he tries any rough stuff, but doan hurt de lady." Evidently the Mexicans understood English, for they nodded and separated, intending to take Nat one on each flank, while the Negro made a frontal attack.

But suddenly the detective and Cora, who kept close to him, made a leap to pass between the Negro and the Mexican on the left of the detective.

At the same moment Nat pretended to look behind, and over the heads of the trio, as if seeing a rescue party and he cried loudly:

"You're just in time, Jake! Take 'em from the back and shoot to kill!"

The ruse worked perfectly, for the Negro and the Mexicans turned, expecting to see a rescue party. At that moment Nat made a rush, pulling Cora after him, and, safely reaching the door of the dungeon, passed between the Negro and one of his helpers.

Turning like a flash, Nat sent a bullet through the dangling electric light. He then pulled shut the door of the dungeon.

"That will give us a few seconds start," he said to Cora. "Come on!"

"Do you know your way out?" she asked.

"Yes," he answered. "There is a secret stair."

He hurried back to the private room where there was to have been a quiet supper for two. The various corridors of the underground part of the club were still lighted.

Nat and his companion entered the room. Further preparations for the meal had been made, for there was food on the table, but no sign of the aged servant.

"Now to escape!" cried Nat.

He pressed the stone that operated the door to the secret stair, and watched it slowly opening. But as the opening widened several loud shouts and screams of fear came from above.

The next moment there was a heavy explosion, as of a bomb, and a shower of bricks, stones and mortar fell upon Nat and the girl. There were a succession of grinding, crashing sounds, and then came darkness in which Nat and his companion seemed buried under an avalanche of dirt and stones.

Nat Ridley felt a stinging blow on his head, and then he knew no more.

CHAPTER XV

IN HIDING

The detective seemed to be walking down a long, dark lane, at the end of which he saw a faint glimmer of light. The light hurt his eyes as it grew brighter and the radiance increased as he came nearer to what, at last, seemed to be the rising sun.

Then, as the pain in his head and eyes became almost unbearable with the nearness of the light, which appeared to sting and burn him, Nat Ridley became aware that he was staring at the rising sun—a ball of golden fire—which shone full in his face, coming through a hole in a pile of stones. Nat found himself half reclining on some burlap bags and, as he tried to sit up, he became aware of a soft hand gently pressing him back while a voice said:

"You had better lie quiet a little longer."

"What happened? Who are you?" asked Nat. Then he saw Cora Ardell looking at him. Her face was grimy and there was a smear of blood on it. But she was still beautiful.

"Oh, now I remember," observed Nat haltingly. "We were in the dungeon and there was some sort of explosion."

"A bomb went off upstairs in the club, I guess," said Cora. "The top of the cellar fell down on us just as you were going to lead me up the secret stairway."

"That's it!" exclaimed Nat, as memory came back to him. He moved his legs and arms, and found, aside from some bruises and stiffness, that he was suffering but little. No bones were broken, but there was still that terrible pain in his head. He put his hand to it and felt a large lump.

"A stone fell on you there, and you were knocked out," explained the girl.

"Then how did I get here?" asked Nat, for he looked about him and saw that he was lying in a sort of tunnel of stone, with open country just beyond. "How did I get here, out of the cellar?"

"I dragged you here," Cora answered.

"What, you—alone?"

"Oh, I am stronger than you think," she went on, with a wavering smile. "And you know it is easier to drag a person than to carry him. I don't believe I could have carried you—in fact, I know I couldn't have done that. But it was comparatively easy after I'd rolled you over on a pile of bags, to keep the stones from hurting you—it was comparatively easy to make a rope of some other bags and haul you along."

"But how did you get me up the stairs?" asked Nat.

"There weren't any stairs left after the explosion," Cora replied. "They tumbled down and made a sort of a runway."

"And you ran up it with me?" questioned Nat, smiling now, as the pain in his head, caused partly by the rush of blood following a return to consciousness, began to ease.

"I didn't do much running," confessed the girl. "I had to do a lot of pulling and hauling. But at last I got you this far and I thought we had better stay here. I couldn't tell who might be after you—and me."

"I guess they'll be after both of us," admitted Nat. "I may as well tell you now that I am a detective who was engaged by your cousin to solve this mystery, just before he, himself, was killed by the Tolas. There is something terrible about their vengeance!"

"I had begun to believe so," admitted Cora. "What are we to do?"

"That will need to be considered," returned Nat. "First, though, let me thank you for saving my life."

"Oh, I don't believe I did that."

"Yes you did!" insisted the detective. "It would have been only a question of time when those Mexicans would have come down in the ruined cellar to look for me. El Capitan had reason for wishing me out of the way. I had a letter of his," and Nat put his hand in his pocket and took out the purloined missive which was still there.

"El Capitan!" murmured the girl.

"Do you know him?"

"I heard the men who kidnapped me speaking of him," Cora answered. "He is the leader, it seems."

"I guessed as much," answered Nat. "Well, so far, we are out of his clutches. Did you see what happened to the two Negroes and their Mexican friends?"

"No. After the explosion everything was dark. But I found a flashlight in your pocket, and when I saw you were alive, but unconscious, I started to get you out of the cellar. I went up the place where the stairs had been, and then I thought this would be a good hiding spot."

"They haven't found us here yet, at any rate," Nat said. "Though it will be only a question of time, I suppose. It is morning, I take it."

"There is the rising sun," Cora confirmed him. "It is breakfast time, but we have nothing to eat."

"And I think we would both be a bit better off for something," stated Nat. "I'm feeling much better now," he went on as he arose and stood up, for the tunnel, in which he had returned to consciousness, was high enough for this. He walked around and was quite himself again.

"Where are you going?" asked Cora as she saw him walking back toward the incline of ruined stairs up which, at more cost and toil then she admitted, she had dragged him.

"I'm going to see if I can rustle some grub, as the saying is," admitted Nat.

"You mean to go back into that dangerous place?" the girl gasped.

"I don't believe it will be particularly dangerous now," Nat answered. "That is, unless it collapses on me, and I guess all the stones that were to fall have come down."

"I was thinking of that Negro and the Mexicans."

"Oh, they're gone!" declared Nat. "You can make up your mind that after such an explosion as that the Paloma police are on the job. We seem to be quite a little distance away from the Cordova Club, but I imagine the place is mostly in ruins and there is probably a cordon of police around it now."

"Then why not appeal to them?" the girl inquired.

Nat Ridley shook his head, then stopped suddenly, for the pain shot back.

"No," he said. "It is best to let the Tola gang think we perished in the ruins. If we went to the police it would soon be known. We will lie low for a time—remain here in hiding. When you're campaigning against an enemy," he went on, "the more you can fool and puzzle and keep him guessing the better. We'll let those Tolas think we're out of the running and then we'll jump in again when they least expect it."

"Then you mean to stay here for a while?"

"Until after dark, at least. We can go out then in comparative safety. But we'll need some water to drink and some food. There was the start of a supper in that room of the secret stairs just before the explosion. I think I can get enough to put us over until night."

"I would like some water," admitted Cora.

"And you need food," added Nat. "You stay here. I won't be gone long."

"Be careful!" she begged him. "These are terrible men!"

He nodded, and then crawled over the uneven pile of stones until he had found the inclined runway up which he had been dragged. When he saw it he marveled that the girl could thus have hauled him to a safe hiding place.

Waiting and listening to make sure the way was clear, and hearing nothing, Nat Ridley made his way down into what, before the explosion, had been the room where the aged servant had greeted him. The table was tipped over and split, rocks and concrete having fallen on it, but from the heap of débris the sleuth managed to salvage some food. Fortunately, he also found an earthen jar of clean water. With this he returned to find Cora anxiously waiting for him.

"I—I thought something happened to you," she faltered.

"Enough has happened, and probably a lot more will," replied Nat lightly. "But I'm all right for the present. Let's eat!"

The sun rose higher, moving away so that the golden beams no longer penetrated the tunnel. The two examined their hiding place and concluded that the tunnel was the secret egress from the Cordova Club cellar—an exit used in times of trouble.

Nat was considering what his next move would be, and Cora was putting away what food was left, in readiness for the next meal, when there was a rattle of fallen stones and a form darkened the hole of the tunnel.

"Someone is coming!" whispered the girl.

CHAPTER XVI

ON TO ROLAMOTAZA

A number of little caves and caverns had been formed in the tunnel with its partial collapse, and Nat Ridley, hearing the approach of someone at the outer end and seeing the darkening of the shaft, acted quickly.

"In here!" he whispered to Cora as he guided her into one of the caves. He thrust himself in after her and the two remained there, scarcely daring to breathe. They listened anxiously and heard voices talking in Spanish.

"I wish I knew what they were saying," whispered Nat. "I can understand some Spanish, and read it and write it, but I want to make no mistake about what they are saying."

"I can tell you," and the girl's voice was as low as his own. "I studied the language before taking this position."

"Good! What are they talking about?"

Cora listened while the voices went on—two of them—and the sound of footsteps could be heard penetrating the tunnel.

"One said," reported the girl, "that it was useless to look in here for that pig of a Bill Brice, the hardware man. I don't know who they mean."

"I do," chuckled Nat. "They mean me."

"But I thought you said your name was Nat Ridley?"

"I assumed a disguise to come here, and also took another name," the detective replied. "I was Bill Brice for a time."

"Then they are looking for you?"

"So it seems. But what else are they saying?"

Cora listened further and once more whispered:

"One seems to think you might be in here and the other doesn't." There was a further exchange of excited Spanish talk and Cora added: "There, the one who says it would be useless to search in here has his way about it—they are going off."

"Good!" softly exclaimed Nat. "I'd hate to have another fight on my hands," and he put his automatic back in his pocket.

The two, crouched in the hole amid the shattered stones, listened and heard the searchers retreating. They had come only a little way into the tunnel.

"I guess we're safe now," murmured Nat. "If no more come until after dark, we'll be out of here."

"Where are we to go?" the girl asked.

"That is something which must be considered," decided Nat. "I must learn more about the double dagger crowd before I will be in a position to arrest any of them. El Capitan is the leader, I think, but I am not sure. As soon as I get out of here I'll make up a little different and scout around. As for you—"

"They will probably be on the lookout for me," interrupted Cora. "Oh, I am so afraid they will kidnap me again!"

"They probably would attempt to get Cora Ardell into their power," admitted Nat. "But I fancy they will have no use for Miss Belle Stanton, the sister of James Stanton, who has come here looking for a ranch to buy."

"Who is James Stanton?" she asked.

"I am going to be," chuckled Nat. "And you are going to be my sister— that is, if you have no objections."

"Of course, I haven't. I need a brother—very much!" and she smiled wanly at him as they moved back toward the exit of the tunnel where the air was fresher.

"Then this is my plan," went on the detective. "When we go out of here, which we will do after night falls, we will so alter our appearances as to look like a man seeking to buy a ranch and his sister who is accompanying him. We will find a quiet boarding place where I can leave you while I scout around a bit."

"But how can you disguise me and yourself?" asked Cora.

Nat took from his pocket a small but very complete make-up box, such as those used by moving picture actors, and explained how he could change Cora's face and his own.

"Our clothes won't matter greatly," he said. "But I can change mine a bit, and I should think, by sort of pinning up your skirt on one side, perhaps making some flounces or ruffles in it—"

"Oh, how did you know so much about dresses?" asked Cora, with a laugh.

"I was married—once," Nat answered in a low voice. "My wife died when my son was a little fellow."

"Oh, I am sorry—forgive me!"

"It is all right," Nat said. "Now to business."

They talked over their plans, and Cora told more, as she remembered it, about the Tola gang. Nat made mental notes of her information. The day wore on, and no more intruders came to the ruined tunnel. The exit from it appeared to be removed some distance from the Cordova Club—or what was left of that organization's headquarters after the bomb explosion.

The two ate again, and drank some more of the water, which kept cool owing to the evaporation properties of the porous jar in which it was contained.

Then as the glow of the sunset was fading, Nat began to disguise himself and the girl, making a much better job of it than was to be expected under the circumstances.

When it was dark the two went out of the tunnel, first having made an observation that showed that the way was clear. They found themselves near a narrow street, or rather, an alley, that led to the main thoroughfare on which the club was, or had been, situated.

"Let's stroll past and see it," proposed Nat.

"Suppose they discover us?"

"In cases like this the bold way is the best," declared Nat. "They would never look for us at the very place where they had had you a prisoner. Come on—it will be perfectly safe."

It was. The clubhouse was not as greatly damaged as Nat and Cora had feared, but it was put out of use as a club, temporarily at least, and, as the detective had surmised, the police were in charge. The two made their way through the curious throng, but there was no sign of El Capitan or any of his men.

A little later "James Stanton" and his sister had secured lodgings in a quiet boarding house, and Nat, venturing back to the hotel where he had left his baggage, claimed it.

He asked the landlady's daughter to go out to buy some clothes for Cora, explaining that he and his sister had come away in a hurry, and there seemed to be no thought but that everything was all right.

Having told Cora not to worry, Nat, in his new character, went scouting about town that evening, frequenting several places where, so he learned, Mexicans, both Spanish and Indian, fond of nightlife, congregated. In one way and another he picked up considerable information about oil wells in general and the Lemberg wells in particular.

"But I wouldn't advise anybody to take stock in those wells," said a grizzled plainsman for whom Nat bought some liquid refreshment while the sleuth himself indulged in a black cigar.

"Why not?" asked Nat. "Not that oil is my line," he added. "I want a ranch."

"And, as I told you," said his companion, "I can put you on to some bargains in that business. But if any of your friends are thinking of buying oil shares, let them lay off the Lemberg derricks."

"Why so?"

"Because it ain't healthy," was the answer. "Too many folks connected with those wells have passed out."

78

Nat was interested, but could glean little of real value from his informant except in a general way, which confirmed his first suspicions. The Tola gang, either from motives of guarding ancient rights or for more worldly reasons, since the borings had proved of such great value, wanted back the wells they had sold.

But certain things which Nat picked up caused him to go to the local telephone exchange a little later that evening, where he put in a long distance call for New York. He knew his talk would not be overheard or cut in on by any outside person if he talked from a booth in the telephone office.

Presently Nat was speaking to Berry Todd and giving that somewhat surprised sleuth some instructions, part of which were to be conveyed to Baldy Stoler.

"Are you all right, Chief?" Berry wanted to know.

"So far," was all Nat said. "I'm counting on you now!"

"And you won't count in vain!" Berry assured him. "We'll soon join you."

When Nat got back to the boarding house he found a note under his door. It was from Cora and said:

"When you come in, no matter what time it is, slip a note under my door saying you are safe. I shall not be asleep."

Nat smiled and scribbled on a leaf of his notebook, going out into the hall to slip it under the girl's door. As he did so he thought he saw a figure slinking away down the corridor—the figure of a man who seemed to have been listening at the girl's door.

In a flash, all of Nat's suspicions returned, and he hurried to the head of the stairs. But there was no one in sight and he thought he was mistaken and that it might have been either the landlady, her daughter, or one of the maids making a usual round of the house to see that all was right.

As Nat slipped the bit of paper under the door he heard Cora's voice asking:

"Are you all right?"

"Quite so," he replied. "And you?"

"All right. Only I fancy someone is watching outside my window."

"Imagination," said the sleuth in a whisper. "You're all right. Go to sleep."

Nat slept soundly, so soundly in fact that he had to be called by the landlady. He had left a message when going out in the evening, that if he was not stirring by eight o'clock he was to be roused. But he was a little surprised when he heard the woman's voice saying:

"It is after eight, sir!"

"I'll be right down to breakfast!" Nat said.

"Is my sister up?"

"Your sister isn't in her room, nor has she been down to breakfast," said the landlady. "Perhaps she went out for an early morning walk. None of us have seen her."

Nat stifled an exclamation of alarm that rose to his lips, and, hurrying into his clothes, went to Cora's room. She was not in it, and there was some indication of confusion about the apartment. The bed had not been slept in, but there was evidence that the girl had stretched out on it without turning back the covers. It seemed she had not undressed.

"She's gone!" exclaimed Nat.

"Has anything happened?" asked the landlady.

"I—I'm afraid so," was the answer. "Was there any disturbance in the night—I mean here in your house?"

"I heard you come in," volunteered the landlady, "and then I heard you go into your sister's room. I heard you talking, and then some time later I thought I heard you and her going out."

"I didn't go into her room," said Nat, trying not to show his excitement. "I spoke to her from outside, that was all. Then I went to bed. But she is gone—she must have gone out after I was asleep."

"Then she went out with some man," said the woman.

"Rather, some man took her out!" cried Nat. "I see it now! They have kidnapped her again, the scoundrels! I thought I saw someone spying at her door when I came in. I wish I had searched farther than I did. Yes, they have kidnapped her again!"

"This is terrible!" gasped the landlady. "I will call the police!"

"No!" Nat stopped her with a gesture. "I will handle this case without the police. I'm a detective."

He told the excited landlady enough to satisfy her, pledged her to secrecy, and then began to examine Cora's room. One of the first things he found was the note he had written her. But scrawled on the back, though not in Nat's writing was the one word—*Rolamotaza*.

"It's a clew she left for me!" mused the sleuth. "The Tola gang have taken her there. Well, it's me for Rolamotaza as fast as a train can take me! The devils! They get ahead of me every time!"

A few hours later Nat Ridley was headed for the Mexican city where the Lemberg oil wells were located.

CHAPTER XVII

INTO THE HILLS

Sun-bronzed and wind-tanned, a lone cowboy rode a pinto pony along the stretch of sand and sagebrush. Now and then, from beneath the flapping brim of his sombrero, he looked at the faint trail ahead of him, and now and then he raised the red handkerchief about his neck and wiped his perspiring face.

"It's a darn long way from here to Times Square," mused the lone cowboy. "But I've got to go through with it now. Go 'long there, you pinto!" he called encouragingly to his steed, and the pony increased its ambling pace.

The sun grew hotter and hotter. It was toward the close of a hot afternoon, and Mexico, the Mexico of the plains, was never noted for coolness.

Presently the rider pulled his horse to a stop and slung around in front of him the canvas covered canteen that had been bobbing against the pinto's flanks and, as he took out the cork and tilted some of the warm, brackish contents down his throat, he murmured:

"Sorry, pony, that there isn't some for you, but there's hardly a hollow tooth full for me. But we may strike the city soon."

The pinto whinnied teasingly as it caught the whiff of water, but there was none for it and the cowboy had soon urged his animal on again. But presently he stopped once more, looked long and earnestly at the trail before him and remarked:

"A sign of life at last. Now if this is somebody besides a Mex maybe I can get some information. Hop to it, pinto!"

The pony pricked up its ears as it saw and smelled another horse approaching and broke into a canter, which caused the cowboy to remark:

"That's better! I guess you smell water." But his cheerfulness vanished as he caught sight of the approaching rider and he remarked: "A Mex again! Can't get any sense out of him—not with what little I know of Spanish. Wish Cora was here!"

The advancing Mexican peon stopped as he saw the cowboy pulling rein and made a greeting in Spanish.

"I don't know what you're saying, stranger," drawled the cowboy, "but I'm pleased to meet you just the same. Now how far is it to town and a good drink of water? I've been traveling a week it seems, though I know it isn't more than a day. Where's this city of yours?"

"No sabe, señor."

"The deuce you don't! Well, I'll have to make motions then, I guess," sighed Pocus Pete. "Look," and he opened his mouth, held up his canteen, pretended to pour out water where there was none and then exclaimed:

"Rolamotaza—where is it at?"

"Oh, Rolamotaza—Rolamotaza!" exclaimed the other, comprehending now, but giving the Spanish name of the town the correct pronunciation. "Pronto! Pronto!"

"You mean I'll get there pronto—soon?" asked Pocus Pete.

The Mexican nodded a vigorous assent, smiled, waved his hand, and called to his bony horse.

"Well, I'm nearer than I thought then," mused the cowboy. "Guess I won't turn back to Times Square. Go on, pinto!"

And to such good speed did he urge his mount that a little later he was guiding the animal down a trail through the hills toward a small, Mexican village, on the outskirts of which loomed the unsightly oil derricks.

"Struck the right place, I guess!" muttered the cowboy. "Now if I can strike somebody that appreciates good, old United States talk I'll be all set."

He rode through the one and only main street of the town, noting that the population consisted of cowboys like himself, Mexicans, Spaniards, Italians, and other foreigners who seemed to be in the oil trade, and a few women and children. Following the crowd, Pocus Pete found himself near a combined hotel, saloon, and gambling hall, evidences of all three branches of trade being well in evidence.

"Say, buddy, can a guy get a feed and something to drink in there?" asked the cowboy of another of his fraternity.

"Surest thing you know. Where you from?"

"Paloma, and looking for a corral," answered Pocus Pete, as he gave his name.

"Well, you've come to a mighty poor place for cattle punchin'," was the comment, as the other announced himself as Lazy Ike Nolan. "It's all oil down here—oil an' Greasers an' sudden death."

"Sudden death!" exclaimed the other. "How come?"

"It ain't healthy to talk about it," was the answer. "But watch your step, that's all. I wish I'd never come to the darn place. I'm broke now and my buddy will be pretty soon if he don't keep away from the gang he's in there with now, tryin' to rub the spots off the cards," and Lazy Ike sighed.

"Maybe you wouldn't take it amiss if I offered to buy you a drink, pardner," suggested Pocus Pete.

"You could do that twice an' not insult me," was the reply. "Lead me to it!"

Pocus Pete tied his pony to the hitching rail in front of the "Stella d'Ora," or Golden Star, as the combined hotel and gambling joint was named, and, having tossed a coin to a boy who was carrying buckets of water to the ponies, with motions to water his steed, Pocus Pete followed his new friend.

There was a bar doing a good business and in a room beyond it several gambling games going on.

"Name your poison," said Pocus Pete to Lazy Ike as they lined up in front of the bar. "It's water for mine until I get soaked up. I had a hot ride."

"Don't blame you, pard," agreed the other. "But I'll have some red licker if it's all the same to you. There he goes—bettin' his last cent I know!" he exclaimed as he poured out a generous drink and looked into the gambling room.

"Who?" asked Pocus Pete.

"My side kick—Slim Jim Burke," was the answer. "I got cleaned out, and I told him to keep away. But he was so darn sure he could get back what I lost and make a clean up that he went in. Now look at him!"

He pointed to a cowboy like himself who was seated at a table with several Mexicans. It was an intense gambling game, as was plainly evident, and a crowd of spectators ringed the participants.

"Let's saunter in and see what kind of hands your pardner is holding," suggested Pocus Pete when he had taken three glasses of water one after the other, to the no small astonishment of the bartender. But when a dollar bill was tossed over the mahogany in payment of the water alone, the whiskey or "red licker," being also paid for, there was a murmur of approval.

"There goes his last dollar—I know the signs," whispered Lazy Ike to his new friend as they neared the poker table. "An' now we're both broke."

It was evident that a final play was being made, and as Pocus Pete watched the dealing he suddenly stepped forward, laid a hand on the shoulder of Slim Jim and exclaimed in a drawling but loud voice:

"Don't bet on this hand, buddy. The deal's crooked. That guy," and he pointed to the Mexican dealer, "is slipping his friend cards from the bottom of the deck. Lay off it!"

At once there was a chorus of excited shouts from the Mexican gamblers—shouts in Spanish—and in the midst of it Lazy Ike called to his "side kick":

"Snap out of it! You're being done!"

Slim pushed back his chair, hardly knowing what it was all about, showing signs of wonder at the interference of the strange cowboy. But the dealer and his gambling friends did more than show wonder.

"Who are you?" roared the dealer in fairly good English, as he glared at Pocus Pete. "How dare you break up our game?"

"Go easy, friend," drawled the other. "Breaking up games when I see a friend of my friend being double-crossed, is one of the best things I do. I saw you dealing off the bottom—like this—"

He reached over, picked up the scattered cards and, with the hands of a master magician, began dealing the cards now from the top and now from the bottom. He turned up the hand he had given the former dealer, showing four kings, but hardly had the murmurs of surprise at this trick died away than Pocus Pete turned over the cards he had dealt to himself, showing four aces.

"It's easy when you know how," he drawled. "But it ain't healthy for them as knows," he added.

The disclosure seemed to sting the Mexican gambler to madness.

"Son of a pig!" he spluttered. "I will show you!"

With a rapid motion he drew a gun, but before he could fire Lazy Ike, whose actions seemed to belie his nickname, had his own weapon out. There were two reports, one following the other, but Lazy Ike had fired first and the Mexican slumped down in his chair, the bullet from his gun singing uncomfortably past the ear of Pocus Pete.

The excitement in the saloon redoubled, and Pocus Pete was drawing his own gun, for there were ugly looks about him, when Lazy Ike called into his ear:

"We'd better beat it now, you an' me an' Slim Jim. They won't leave enough of us to put on a shutter as soon as they get into action. I guess maybe I've croaked that guy."

"Where are you going?" asked Pocus Pete as he allowed himself to be urged out of the place between Lazy Ike and Slim Jim.

"We've got to take to the hills," answered Ike. "It won't be safe for us in town."

It appeared that it was not going to be safe for the trio right then and there, in the Stella d'Ora, for as the three neared the door they found their passage blocked by a number of Mexicans.

"Pigs! Dogs!" hissed the dark-featured men, some of whom were far from sober.

"Kill the Gringoes!" someone yelled.

A big man, whose face showed his passion, rushed at Pocus Pete with a long knife upraised.

"Watch yourself, buddy!" yelled Ike.

There was a sharp report, a little cloud of smoke seemed to float out of the side pocket of Pete's coat, and the Mexican slumped down to the floor.

"Another one down and out!" yelled Ike, the lust of battle in his eyes. "Now we sure got to make a run for it!"

"That was a slick shot," muttered Slim Jim. "Though who you are an' how Ike picked you up, I don't know."

"An' this ain't no time to ask questions, either!" sung out Ike. "Come on! Take it on the jump!"

The three ran from the saloon, leaped to their ponies at the hitching rail and galloped off.

"To the hills!" cried Lazy Ike. "We'll stick by you, Pocus Pete!"

As they galloped through the town the hoof-beats of their horses were punctuated with the shots from many guns, while bullets sang an ominous, whining song over their heads.

CHAPTER XVIII

THE BLACK CAVE

"You fellows know this country better than I do," remarked Pocus Pete as he guided his pinto pony out among the hills that led away from the Mexican town where they had just escaped from the gambling den. "I'll have to depend on you to get me out of here."

"Don't worry about that," drawled Lazy Ike whose speech was, at times, as slow as his actions. "We'll stick by you to the last."

"Though, for the matter of that," went on the strange cowboy, "those fellows who were juggling the pasteboards didn't get any more than was coming to 'em."

"You're darn right!" chimed in Slim Jim. "Say, pard, I gotta hand it to you for shufflin' the cards! How'd you work it?"

"Just a trick," and Pocus Pete smiled. "But say, do you fellows know where you are and where we're goin'?"

"You well said it!" exclaimed Lazy Ike, flapping his pony with the reins. "We know this country all right, an' to our sorrow. I wish we'd never crossed the Rio Grande."

"Same here," came sorrowfully from his pal.

"What's wrong with it?" asked Pocus Pete. "Too much oil?"

"Too much oil for a cattleman," answered Slim Jim. "An' there's other things, too."

"What other things?" asked the pinto-riding cowboy curiously. He acted as though he had long been on the trail of something or somebody and that now he was nearing the end of his quest. "What other things?"

"You tell him, Slim," urged Lazy Ike. "We got to stick together now, since that shootin' fracas, so he might as well know what's what."

"Yes," remarked Pocus Pete, "if the cops get after us we're all in the same boat, I reckon, though you didn't shoot anybody, Jim."

"Not this time. But I gotta couple of notches on my gun handle," boasted the cowboy. "Not but what the fellows who stopped my bullets didn't get what they deserved," he added. "I'm no promisc'us shooter. It was them or me, an' I'd ruther it'd be them. So the cops, as you call 'em, are after me, too—only they haven't got onto my curves yet back there in Rolamotaza."

"Cops," drawled Lazy Ike meditatively. "I ain't heard that word in a long spell. You must 'a' been East recent, Pocus Pete."

"I'm from the East, originally," admitted the cowboy on the pinto. "Some of the words stick to me yet. I reckon they ain't got no regular police out here, have they?"

"These Greasers? Naw!" exclaimed Slim Jim as he shoved a big wad of tobacco into his mouth. "Con-stab-u-lary—that's what they call 'em in Mex. Dirty, greasy Greasers—that's all!"

"But they shoot without stoppin' to ask why or wherefor," warned Lazy Ike. "So we'd best put a few miles between them an' us afore Don Juan Castro starts the ball game."

"Don Juan Castro?" exclaimed Pocus Pete, and there was so much excitement in his voice that his two companions looked at him in surprise and Jim asked:

"You know him?"

"I've heard of him," was the answer. "He's a big cattle man, isn't he?"

"Naw! Oil," and Jim got rid of some of his tobacco juice. "He owns a lot of oil wells around here an' he's always tryin' to git more. There's some wells here owned by a party out your way—in the East, I mean—N' York, I heard. Well, this Don Castro and his gang are after them wells."

"They tried to buy 'em," added Ike. "An' when they couldn't do that, well, some queer things begun happenin'."

"That's what I was goin' to tell you about," put in Slim. "This country ain't no good for cattle—it's all oil, an it ain't healthy for them as dabbles in oil, 'less they're in right with Don Castro."

"What happens?" asked Pocus Pete.

"They passes out—sudden like," answered Slim and he made a motion as if sticking a knife into someone. "An' that ain't the worse of it, neither," he went on.

"No?" questioned Pocus Pete.

"No, sir! There's signs that them as passes out sudden has been done away with by a secret society. There was certain signs left near each dead man, an' three was killed lately to my certain knowledge."

"That's right," chimed in Lazy Ike. "Three!"

"What was the mysterious sign?" asked Pocus Pete.

"It was a sign of a double dagger drawed on a card found near the dead men," resumed Slim. "An' in one of the bodies, a regular double dagger was found—a knife with a big blade on one end an' a small blade on the other. Looked like if they didn't get you goin' they would comin' or visse versy as they used to say when I went to school."

"So they found the double dagger in one of the victims, did they?" asked Pocus Pete.

"It was left stickin' in one of the stiffs, if that's what you mean," chuckled Lazy Ike.

"Where it is? Who has it? I mean where is that double dagger now?" and Pocus Pete showed so much excitement that both his new friends looked at him in wonder. Then Slim added:

"It didn't stay in him long. Feller named Steele, it was. An' he got steel —cold steel—poor slob! This is how it come about. Ike an' me we moseyed down here lookin' for work, an' when we found it weren't no cattle country we sort of stuck around, pickin' up odd jobs. It wasn't so bad at first, though we didn't have no great hankerin' for oil. An' then the queer killin's begun.

"But about this double dagger you seems to be interested in. One mornin' a young feller we happened to know—he was a college boy who'd run away an' he got a job down here. He used to ride off by himself a lot, alone. One mornin' he come racin' back to town, his pony all a lather of foam, sayin' he'd seed a dead man out in the gully, an' he had a double dagger stuck in his heart. That's how it was knowed the killin's was done with that kind of a knife."

"So they found the double dagger, did they?" asked Pocus Pete.

"Well, Jimmie Dale—that was this college lad's name, saw the knife stickin' in poor Steele," went on Slim. "But when some of us went out there with a few of what passes for police around here, the knife was gone."

"Who took it?"

"Nobody could tell. Likely it was some of them that drove the double dagger into Steele's heart. They must 'a' knifed him and then got a scare that sent 'em off on the run 'fore they had time to pull the knife out. Then they come back an' got it."

"Looks as if they cared a lot for it," commented Pocus Pete.

"Reckon so," came from Ike. "Well, now you know what sort of country you've drifted to, Pete, an' I hope you like it."

"I've been in worse places," was the cool answer. "If there is food and water to be had up in these hills I reckon we can hold out."

"Oh, there won't be no trouble about that," declared Slim. "We know a few places to hide."

"The black cave, for one," suggested his pal.

"That's right. We'd better head for that."

"As for grub," went on Ike, "there are a lot of Mexican farmers up in these hills, an' they'll sell us skinny chickens an' them fried beans they call frijoles or tortillas or somethin' like that. An' there's plenty of springs, so we'll make out all right."

"Then we'll camp for a while," suggested Pocus Pete. "As it's my fault, in a way, that you were forced to flee—vamoose you know—" He seemed to have, for the moment, swung out of the cowboy slang. "As it was my doin's that you had to come here you'll let me buy the grub."

"Don't know's we'll have much objection to that," said Slim. "We're about broke."

"That's right," nodded Ike. "But how do you figger it's your fault, Pocus Pete, that we're here because of you?"

"Well, if I hadn't butted in on that card game when I saw Slim being double-crossed—"

"Forgit it!" broke in the cowboy gambler. "I was jest gittin' wise to their game myself, an' I'd likely have started somethin' if you hadn't. No, we're all in the same boat, an' we'll stick together."

The trio rode on. The ponies were fleet, and soon took them beyond pursuit, which, as a matter of fact, did not last long. Perhaps the Mexicans did not relish the quick shooting of the cowboys.

They rode up among the hills and stopped at a farm, run by a peon and his wife, where Pocus Pete footed the bill for food—it was not a costly meal, a dollar buying enough for all three.

That night they camped in the open, rolled in blankets near a fire, and the next morning traveled on, for Ike and Slim said the black cave, a natural cavern in the hills, would be reached about noon.

The sun was not yet at the zenith when Lazy Ike, pointing ahead on the trail, drawled:

"There she is!"

"What?" asked Pocus Pete.

"The black cave."

The newly arrived cowboy glanced to a dark opening in the side of the hill, and, as he looked, he said in a low voice:

"Somebody's ahead of us."

"What do you mean?" asked Slim.

"I mean there are some fellows in the black cave. What had we better do, boys? This is your game."

Lazy Ike and Slim Jim peered from beneath their sombreros at some horsemen coming out of the cavern.

CHAPTER XIX

PURSUED

"What you reckon that means, Ike?" questioned Slim Jim.

"Doggoned if I know. Looks like somebody had preëmpted our claim, don't it?"

"Somethin' like that," agreed the other.

"Are you two guys supposed to have a claim on this black cave?" asked Pocus Pete as the three reined in their horses and stood looking at the other cavalcade of riders—perhaps half a dozen—who came out of the cavern as if aroused at the sight of the trio.

"No, we ain't got no more of a claim than anybody else," said Ike. "But Slim an' me, we sort of found this cave when we first come to this oil region, and we lived in it a few days when we was sort of gettin' the lay of things. We've often been back to it between times, but never before did we see anybody in it."

"That's right!" chimed in his friend.

"An' now there's a mob here," went on Pocus Pete. "It must mean something."

"It does!" agreed Lazy Ike. "An' I don't like the looks of it."

"Same here," mused his pal. "An' would you look at that!" he exclaimed as there was a movement among the horsemen at the black cave. "I'll be darned if they ain't headin' our way!" he cried.

It was so. The six horsemen urged their steeds to a trot along the trail toward Pocus Pete and his two friends.

"They're after us!" cried Jim.

"Sure as you're a foot high!" echoed his pal.

"What had we better do?" asked Pocus Pete as he took out his automatic.

"No, don't shoot," advised Jim. "We wouldn't stand much chance against twice our number. Those aren't Greasers. They're some of the gang that hangs around the Stella Dora," so he pronounced the name of the Golden Star café. "They can shoot."

"You mean they are some of Don Castro's gang?" asked Pocus Pete.

"You got me! We'd better give 'em a run for their money."

So, turning their horses about, the three raced along the trail they had come, while, with shouts that had anger in them, the other horsemen took up the pursuit. A few shots rang out, the bullets whizzing uncomfortably close to the heads of Pocus Pete and his friends.

"Ain't that jest the rottenest luck!" exclaimed Jim as he leaned over his pony's neck to give less of a target to their enemies.

"Sure is!" agreed his pal. "I figgered on takin' it easy in that cave for a while, an' now we got to sweat leather again. Well, I guess we can beat 'em at that."

"They aren't catching up to us, at any rate," observed Pocus Pete. "Our horses are fresher than theirs, I take it."

"You take it right, friend," admitted Slim Jim.

"Have you any idea where you are heading for now?" went on Pete.

For a few moments the three rode on without this question being answered. The pursuers, though distanced at first, were still coming on, and, though hidden by turns in the trail, the pattering of their horses' feet could still be heard.

"Yes, where you aim to pull up, Slim?" asked Ike.

"What about the Indian's Nose?" asked Slim.

"Not bad. It's a good place to camp, an' we can see a good ways off when anybody's comin'. How does that strike you, Pocus Pete?"

"Well, I guess," was the answer as the new cowboy urged his pinto pony along. "I'm a stranger here. I'll have to leave it to you. But if it means goin' among the Indians—"

"It's only a name of a mesa about twenty miles farther on," was the answer. "It's elevated land, a fine place to camp, water an' everything. A little game to shoot, too. An' you can look for a mile or two each way so you can see when anybody's comin' to make trouble. What say?"

"I say let's head there, if we can shake these fellows off," said Pocus Pete with a look back. But the pursuers were not in sight.

"Snap into it!" called Ike, and the three rode on. But ever as they made a turn in the trail among the hills, they could hear the men from the black cave coming behind them. It was not until nearly noon that they lost the sound, and then Ike said:

"Guess we can take it a bit easy now. There's two or three forks in the road that we passed an' those fellows may have taken one."

"In that case we can let our horses rest," suggested Pocus Pete, for it was high time they pulled rein.

They found a spring of water and with the food they had brought with them from the Mexican farm they drank and made a meal, feeling much better after that.

Then, as they were preparing to mount again and keep on to the Indian's Nose, Pocus Pete arrived at a decision. He looked sharply at his two companions and said:

"Boys, I've got something to tell you."

"Spill it," laconically advised Jim.

"I'm not a cowboy," was the next statement.

"We knowed that long ago!" chuckled Ike.

"An' as long as you ain't the sheriff, we don't give a darn!" went on his partner.

"How'd you know I wasn't what I pretended to be?" asked Pete curiously. "By the way I ride?"

"No, you ride pretty darn good, if you ask me," said Ike.

"It's the breaks you make in speakin' now an' again," said his companion. "An' 'cops'! Bust me for a wall-eyed pike, soon as you said 'cops' I knowed you wasn't no cowboy—at least, not from around here. But you don't have to tell us, mister. We ain't cravin' to know your secret. We got some of our own."

"But I want to tell you," went on the other. "I don't like the way things are breaking down here. And I don't like the way those men from the black cave are coming after us. Something may happen. A stray bullet might just clip me, and—"

"You're right there," admitted Slim Jim gravely. "So if you got anythin' on your conscience—"

"Oh, it isn't that," and Pocus Pete laughed. "But the ends of justice might suffer if I happened to be killed and no one knew who I was or why I came here."

"Then you're the sheriff after all?" and Ike and his chum looked a bit reproachfully at their companion.

"No, I'm not the sheriff, and I'm not after you fellows. I'm Nat Ridley, a private detective from New York, and I'm down here to avenge the murder of a fellow detective—Dan Steele!"

"By thunder!" voiced Ike vigorously.

"A detective!" gasped Slim. "Whatchu know about that!"

"And I'm on the trail of the double dagger gang—Don Castro among them," went on Nat. "Can I count on you to help me?"

For an instant the two cowboys hesitated—but for an instant only. Then with one voice they exclaimed:

"You sure can!" And they held out their bronzed hands.

But a moment later Ike added:

"If we're goin' to help you the best advice I can give you now is to beat it right now!"

"Why?" asked Nat Ridley, alias Pocus Pete.

"Because them fellers are after us again!"
The others listened and heard once more the tattoo of hoof-beats.

CHAPTER XX

OVER THE CLIFF

Leaping into their saddles again, the three horsemen were soon pounding down the trail and away from their pursuers, who seemed to be coming on after them relentlessly.

"They must be powerful anxious to meet up with us," drawled Lazy Ike as he rode beside Nat Ridley.

"They are—for more reasons than one, I fancy," replied the detective. "It isn't altogether the row in the gambling den that makes them want to catch us, though we did put two of their men out of the running."

"Then they want you more than they do us?" asked Ike as he urged his well-going pony to a faster pace.

"That's it. And if you boys want to slide off the trail and let me lead these fellows a chase alone, don't hesitate," suggested Nat.

"What the blazes do you think we are?" snapped out Jim. "We ain't Greasers!"

"I should say not!" cried his pal. "Leavin' a buddy in the lurch ain't our style!"

"I didn't think it was," said Nat Ridley quietly. "But I thought it only fair to give you the chance."

"Well, don't give us no more chances like that," ordered Jim.

"We don't like 'em!" echoed Ike.

And the three rode on.

The two cowboys, in spite of the fact that they were rather loose livers, free spenders, and not very provident, seemed to know their business, which was riding and picking out a good trail. During the period they had been in Mexico they had made good use of their time and knew considerable about the country. It was to them, more than to anything else, that Nat Ridley owed what success he had in this trail after the double dagger gang.

The one and only thing in favor of the detective and the two cowboys was that they had better horses than those ridden by the men who had come out of the black cave.

"What I think is this," said Nat when his two companions asked him how he "figgered out" the gang got to the cavern ahead of them. "The crowd in the gambling joint must have known that you two boys were in the habit of hiding in that cave. Then when you lit out with me, they naturally reasoned that we'd make for here. They must have taken a short cut to get here ahead of us."

"There ain't no short cut!" declared Ike.

"If there was we'd 'a' taken it," added Jim. "Most like they pushed their horses on hard to beat us, an' that's why the ponies ain't goin' so fast now."

"Perhaps," admitted Nat.

"That's it, sure!" declared Lazy Ike. "An' lucky we kept our mounts pretty fresh. Well, we're sure runnin' 'em now," he added, and, indeed, it was calling on all the reserve in the ponies to make them trot along the trail which now led upward.

But luck was still with the trio in advance, and it was not long before they had distanced their pursuers and could pull up their ponies for a breathing spell, which was badly needed. The three men dismounted and picketed the animals in a little glade, where Ike found a spring. But the heated horses were not allowed to drink at once, though it was with the utmost difficulty they were held back until they had cooled off a bit.

Then when they had been allowed to slake their thirst and the three were resting, Nat Ridley told a little more about himself and his mission in Mexico.

"Besides being on the trail of the murderers of the three Lemberg men and my friend Dan Steele," said the detective, "I want to save a girl they kidnapped."

"A girl!" exclaimed the two cowboys.

"Yes, a Miss Cora Ardell," and Nat related the finding of the girl in the dungeon, being beaten by a Negress, and how the two had escaped.

"But they kidnapped her, right out from under my nose, you might say," went on the detective. "It wouldn't do my reputation much good to have that generally known," he admitted, with a wry smile. "But it happened, worse luck. And except for the fact that Miss Ardell left a scrawl, indicating that the scoundrels had brought her to Rolamotaza and of some things she told me in the States, I wouldn't know where to look, though I might have picked up the trail later."

"You say that pretty girl is here?" asked Ike, and, unconsciously, he began to knot his neck handkerchief more carefully.

"I think she was brought to that Mexican town," went on Nat. "But I had no chance to look for her before that row in the saloon started, and we've been kept on the jump ever since."

"On the jump is right," admitted Ike. "But I think we'll get to Indian's Nose soon, and then we can laugh at 'em."

"I'm not so sure of that," said Jim. "But we'll have a better chance, anyhow. Why are those Tola devils after the girl?" he wanted to know.

"She owns a share in the oil wells the Mexicans want to get back," stated Nat. "She was also the secretary of her cousins, the Lembergs, and she may have certain papers which, if the rascals could get them, would aid them in regaining possession of the wells. And now they have Miss Ardell in their power again, and I don't know how to help her."

"Just wait," advised Jim. "Soon as we can give these fellows the slip we'll swing around, cross over the Border, and get a posse of good old cowboys who'll come back and clean out this gang."

"I wish that might happen," replied Nat Ridley. "But I'm afraid we'll have a lot of trouble and be in some danger before that comes to pass. These fellows are as cruel and relentless as their ancient Aztec ancestors."

They pushed on to such good advantage after their rest, during which Nat took occasion to ask his new friends to send word to the Times Square office should the detective be killed and the others escape, that when night came they were in a lonely region, where many trails crossed and the cowboys gave it as their opinions that the pursuers could never follow.

"They can't pick out which trail we took not even if they had a detective like you, Mr. Ridley, to help them!" declared Ike.

"Not in a thousand years!" agreed Slim Jim Burke.

"So much the better for us," said Nat.

That night they slept in the barn of another Mexican farmer, for whose benefit, should he be questioned later, they used false names and talked of searching for a stray bunch of horses. At the farmer's house they bought food and ate heartily.

The night was one of anxiety because, in spite of the confusion of trails, it was possible that Don Castro and his crowd might come upon them. Nat explained his previous encounters with this one of several plotters, and also mentioned El Capitan.

"We've heard of him," said Ike.

"And no good, either," added Jim.

However, the night passed peacefully, and in the morning, after a hearty breakfast and having purchased a supply of food to last for several days, they again took the trail.

Several times at favorable places during the forenoon they stopped to look back and also to listen, but they neither saw nor heard any signs of pursuit and they began to feel that they had distanced their enemies.

It was just getting dusk when Slim, who was riding in advance, gave a shout that sent the blood pumping faster into Nat Ridley's heart.

"What is it?" called the detective anxiously.

"Indian's Nose," was the reply. "We're there!"

A little later the three rode out on a mesa, which made a good place to camp and also, because of the nature of the country, afforded a long outlook to the south, whence pursuit, if any, must come.

"What's to the north?" asked Nat, as they prepared to camp for the night in a little grove of trees.

"The jumpin' off place," answered Ike.

"He means the mesa ends there, and there's a high cliff as straight as a chimney that drops down to the trail at the foot of the mesa," explained Jim.

"Oh," mused Nat. "Well, I hope we aren't chased off this plateau."

"Not much danger, I reckon," said Jim. "They won't find us here."

The night passed peacefully, and they were just finishing breakfast the next morning when Ike, who had gone to see that the horses were all right where they had been picketed, came running back, much excited and shouting:

"They're coming!"

"Who?" asked Nat.

"Don Castro's gang or somebody he's sent after us! They're comin' up the gully, and if we want to get past we've got to fight!"

Hardly had he spoken when around a bend several horsemen appeared, many of whom carried rifles or shotguns. Not expecting the approach of the enemy so soon, the three had not begun to keep a watch, and the Mexicans had stolen up on them in the darkness of the early morning hours.

The mesa, though elevated, was long and narrow, like a nose, after which it was named, and the approach to the camping place of Nat and the cowboys was through a gully, so narrow that not more than three could ride abreast. Now this defile was fairly choked with the approaching horsemen.

"What are we going to do?" asked Ike, as he saw the desperate nature of their chances.

"Fight 'em!" snarled Slim Jim Burke.

"They'd wipe us out!" murmured Nat Ridley. "I'm no coward, as I guess you know," he went on, while the others exclaimed:

"We'll say you aren't!"

"But it would be madness to ride at them in that narrow place," went on the detective. "We might shoot our way through, but, more likely, one or all three of us would be riddled. And I don't want to pass out before I've saved that girl and made the Tola gang pay some of their debts."

"Then what'll we do?" asked Jim.

"How high is that cliff?" asked Nat.

"Too high to jump down, and no pony could slide it," said Ike.

"I don't intend to jump, and we'll have to abandon the horses," went on Nat. "But I guess it isn't too far to get over by using our lariats, is it?"

"The ropes! By jingo, I never thought of that!" cried Ike.

"We can do it!" exclaimed his pal. "And they can't follow, for I don't believe there's a rope in their outfit. They aren't cattlemen. By thunder, Mr.

Detective, you've struck it!"

"We'll go over the cliff!" exulted Ike.

"Fasten the ropes together then," advised Nat, drawing his automatic, and dropping down behind a rock.

"What are you going to do?" asked Jim.

"Give 'em a few shots to hold 'em back until you can make ready," was the answer. "If they rushed us at the last minute we wouldn't have a chance. But I think the bushes will screen our movements until we are ready. Hop to it now, boys!"

The cowboys ran to get their ropes from their saddle horns, and soon came back with the three lariats. Ike stopped in his tracks and exclaimed:

"But look here, Mr. Ridley! We got to shinny down these ropes, you know! Nobody can't lower us. And when the last man is down the ropes will still be hangin' to whatever we fasten 'em to."

"That's so," added Jim, for a moment discouraged. "I never thought of that. We'll have to leave the rope for these devils, an' they'll come down after us."

"No they won't!" declared Nat. "We'll use a double rope, putting the turn of it around that stunted tree on the edge of the cliff. When we are all three down we'll pull one end of the rope and it will slide off and fall down. We won't leave any for them to use."

"By thunder, I never thought of that!" gasped Ike. "Come on, Slim!"

A moment later the two were preparing the way of escape over the cliff while Nat Ridley, kneeling behind a clump of bushes amid the rocks, began firing on the horsemen who were urging their steeds up the rocky defile.

Could he hold them back long enough? That was what Ike and Jim were wondering as they hurriedly knotted together the three strong lassoes.

CHAPTER XXI

A SHOT IN TIME

Nat Ridley's shots in the direction of the advancing Mexicans had hardly ceased rattling amid the rocks of the defile on top of the mesa when the detective hastened toward the edge of the cliff whereon grew a single stunted tree, but strong enough for the ropes to be looped over, thus supporting the men as they went down hand over hand.

"Are you ready?" asked Nat as he saw Jim, who had been kneeling beside his chum, arise.

"Just got 'em all hooked up," was the answer.

"How about you?" asked Ike. "Did you hit any of 'em?"

"A few, I think," answered Nat grimly. He spoke the truth, for his bullets had found marks, bringing to their knees several of the Tola gang, though the sleuth fired to wound and not to kill.

"Snap into it now!" cried Ike. "We haven't any time to lose."

"That's right!" agreed Jim. "They're coming!"

Indeed, down the defile could be heard the ringing of the steel shoes of the horses on the hard rocks.

But by this time the combined lassoes were rigged and, by leaning over the cliff, it could be noted that they extended in a double line to the bottom where a road wound off through the trees and bushes.

"Who's to go first?" asked Slim, as the three paused for a moment on the edge.

"Let Mr. Ridley," suggested Lazy Ike, with his usual drawl. It was noticed that since Nat had revealed his identity the cowboys, having learned who he was, were much less free and easy with him.

"Sure—he goes first!" agreed Jim.

"No," objected Nat. "Without wanting to boast, I may say I'm a better shot than either of you. So if it comes to a rush I can pick off more with my automatic than you can with your guns," and he slipped another full magazine in his weapon.

"There's truth in that," said Ike. "Well, then, Slim, it's between you and me."

"Snap into it!" ordered Nat. "Here, you go first," he ordered Slim Jim, as being the faster of the two. "Then Ike can slide down and I'll follow.

Quick!"

The others were willing to abide by the detective's decision and a moment later the languid cowboy was hanging to the lariats and had slipped over the edge of the cliff. He went down quickly, and his chum was half way to the bottom when the nearer approach of horses and the sound of voices told Nat that the Mexicans were coming on fast.

"Hurry!" advised Nat, and Ike went so fast he blistered his hands, hard as they were.

Nat Ridley, thrusting his automatic into a fold of his coat, to have it in instant readiness, now began the descent. As his head and shoulders disappeared below the edge of the cliff, the first of the pursuers came into view.

"There he is! The dog! The pig!" cried someone in Spanish-accented English.

"Ah, there spoke Don Castro, or I am mistaken!" chuckled Nat.

Suddenly, after having lowered his head over the rim of the cliff, the detective raised himself again, holding on by one hand and by twisting the ropes around his legs. Then he sent several shots into the ranks of the Mexicans, making a hit with each report.

There were yells of rage and cries of pain, and having thus forced the advancing horsemen to a temporary halt, Nat began the descent.

"Stop him! Get the pig! Cut the rope!" yelled Don Castro.

But before this could be done Nat had reached the end of the lariats and had joined Ike and Jim, who stood anxiously waiting.

"Did they shoot at you?" asked Jim.

"No, I peppered them," answered Nat.

He pulled quickly on one side of the double rope, thus slipping it loose from around the anchoring tree, and as the free end rose, the face of a Mexican appeared at the top of the cliff and his hands made an endeavor to snatch the combined lariats before they could fall. It was evident the pursuers had no ropes of their own to use in making the descent.

But Nat, with a quick jerk, pulled the lassoes off the tree, and the coils fell at his feet. Then, calling to Ike and Jim to run on, the detective took a shot at the man above him. A howl of pain succeeded the crack of the automatic and the sleuth knew he had clipped his man. Two Mexicans shot in return, but nobody was hit.

"We're safe now for a time," remarked Ike, with a sigh of relief.

"I hope so," assented Nat. "But where are we going?"

"We can't go far without horses," remarked Jim with a sorrowful air. "A cowboy without a pony is like a sailor without a ship."

"We may be able to pick up something to straddle before very long," said Nat. "I'd be very glad to buy some extra horses if we could find them."

"Gee, you're a sport!" vowed Ike.

"This is business," declared the sleuth. "What are our chances?"

"Well, we may strike a ranch where we can get three broncos," said Slim. "But they won't be much good. No worse, though, than the nags on which they've been riding after us. Gee, I sure do hate to lose my pony!"

"I'll see that you get another," promised Nat. "But if we have to walk, aren't we likely to be overtaken by those fellows, even if they have very poor horses?" he asked.

"I'm not worrying about that," declared Jim. "There's no trail down off the mesa short of half a day's ride, and they aren't going to try the cliff, I guess. No, we're safe for a time."

Then the three began walking along. They were soon lost to view in a grove of trees so that there was no danger of those on the cliff shooting at them, and then they plodded on.

All the rest of that day they marched, halting only when the sun was hottest. They found another Mexican farmer who supplied them with food, and at night they reached a small village where they stayed for the night in an unoccupied adobe hut. But their quest for horses was unavailing.

"Better luck to-morrow," suggested Nat as they rolled in their blankets, for they had brought their packs with them when they slid down the rope at the cliff.

The detective's prophecy was borne out a little later, for a traveling horse-dealer came into the village the next day and offered to sell three steeds at prices which the cowboys said were outrageous.

"This is no time to haggle," declared Nat in an aside. "We want to get back to Rolamotaza. I've got to do what I can to save Miss Ardell."

So the ponies were purchased, together with saddles and bridles, and though Jim and Ike bewailed the fact that the animals were nothing like the ones they had lost, still it was the best that could be done under the circumstances.

Once more mounted, the three, having purchased food, started off, intending to head back to the village to which Cora Ardell had indicated she was being taken by her abductors.

How it happened none of them knew, least of all Nat Ridley, but toward the evening of the third day after their escape over the edge of the cliff, the three were riding down a trail amid the hills, and, rounding a turn, Ike suddenly exclaimed:

"Look where we are!"

"By jinks! What do you know about that?" cried Jim.

"Where are we?" asked Nat.

"On the trail back to the cave!"

"You mean the black cave?"

"Surest thing you know! Say, this is luck!"

"Maybe not so much as you think," suggested the detective. "If that same gang is in there—"

"They're out. They're after us!" chuckled Ike. "This is the best ever!"

"Are you sure you're right?" asked Nat, as the two compared notes about landmarks.

"Certain sure!" answered Ike. "We'll be at the cave in ten minutes. This is the back trail leading to it."

In even less than the time mentioned the two cowboys gave shouts of delight and pointed to the same dark hole in the overhanging rocks that Nat had viewed several days before.

Slim Jim kicked his pony in the sides to spur it forward and approached the cave with a rush. But, just as he reached it, to the horrified surprise of Nat and Ike, a Mexican rushed out, thrust a long pole between the legs of Jim's horse, bowling that none too steady animal over, and bringing the rider to the ground.

With a yell of rage, the Mexican, raising aloft a long knife, rushed at the prostrate man, who was stunned from the fall. And, with a thrill of terror, Nat Ridley recognized in the Mexican's hand the dreaded double dagger.

"Look out, Slim!" yelled Ike. But his shout did no good.

Like a flash, Nat Ridley drew his automatic and fired in the nick of time. As the report rang out, the Mexican, with a shriek of pain and rage, dropped the two-pointed knife from a hand that was reddened with blood.

Nat had shot the weapon from the assassin's fingers, and not a moment too soon. A second later and it would have been buried in Slim's heart.

CHAPTER XXII

THE TOLA EMBLEM

But if the detective and the cowboys with him thought they could silence this raging Mexican with one shot, they were soon to find out to the contrary.

"Dogs and pigs!" hissed the man as he leaped to his feet, for the shock of the bullet in his right hand had sent him spinning around so that he fell. "Pigs!"

"Seems to be their pet word!" chuckled Nat, as he eyed the fellow.

The detective did not give the Mexican credit enough for brute courage and indominable grit. But no sooner was the Mexican on his feet than he made a rush for the double dagger that had fallen to the ground near Slim.

"Grab that knife!" yelled Ike, sensing the fellow's intention.

But Slim was still dazed by the fall from his tripped horse, and not capable of action. It might yet have gone hard with him had not Nat Ridley fired again.

This time the sleuth did not risk shooting at the hand which held the double-pointed knife—the left. It appeared that the Mexican could use either fist for stabbing. Instead Nat aimed at his head.

Such an accurate shot was the detective that he could have sent a bullet through the assassin's head, but he was more merciful than was the member of the Tola gang, and only shot off one ear.

As the bullet gave him this injury, the Mexican, with a scream of terror and pain, dropped the double dagger the second time and then fled down the road that ran in front of the black cave.

"That's the last we'll see of him!" cried Ike.

"There may be more," observed Nat. "Get your gun ready while I go take a look at Slim."

Ike drew his heavy revolver, but no others of the gang came from the cavern, and while Ike stood guard Nat bent over the stunned cowboy. Luckily he was only stunned, and when he had recovered the wind that had been knocked out of him he looked up at Nat, started to rise and murmured:

"Thanks, old man. Hope I can do the same for you some day."

"I don't want to be in as tight a place as that," remarked Nat. "I like a little bigger margin."

"I sure thought he had you!" exclaimed Ike while Nat walked to where the emblem of the Tola gang had been dropped by the murderous Mexican and picked up the double dagger.

"A nasty weapon," observed Slim as he got to his feet, little the worse for his fall. The horse was not hurt, and after scrambling up and running on a little way, was now cropping grass. "He sure did me a dirty fall," he added, dusting off his clothes.

"You're lucky," commented Ike. "Mr. Ridley fired just in time. Look out, sleuth," he added as he heard the detective give a surprised exclamation. "Cut yourself?" he asked.

"No," Nat answered. "But this is a trick dagger. Look here!"

He held out in his hand what seemed to be only the handle of a knife. Both blades had disappeared. But, as the cowboys watched, the shining points of steel sprang into view again.

"What's the idea?" asked Ike.

"The blades appear and disappear by pressure on a spring hidden here," Nat said, indicating where, amid the carving on the handle, a little head of a grinning Aztec god appeared. "Look!"

The detective worked the mechanism, which he had discovered by accident, causing the blades to shoot out and in with a sinister suggestion of the injuries they could cause in the hands of a Tola.

"That's a bad knife," remarked Ike.

"The Tolas have a miniature one like it, which they use as a pin to fasten their cards on the bodies of their victims," Nat informed his friends. "The points of the little dagger are doped in some way so the person about to be murdered is rendered helpless."

"Better look out that the points of that double dagger aren't smeared with dope," advised Slim.

"I'll be careful," Nat promised. "I'll sheath the blades before I put it in my pocket," and he suited his action to his words.

"What are you going to do with it?" asked Slim.

"I don't know yet," was the answer. "But I have an idea that with it I can get hold of some of the secrets of the Tola gang. Now at last we're at the cave where we wanted to hide. But I am in two minds about it. Since getting this dagger, I have half a notion to go back to Rolamotaza and have a look for Miss Ardell."

"Let's rest a bit," suggested Slim. "I don't feel as chipper as I might."

"Oh, I didn't mean to rush off now," remarked Nat. "We'll spend the night here in the cave."

"Maybe we'd better find out first," suggested Ike, "whether there are any more of the gang in there."

"It is hardly likely," said Nat. "They would have come out after what has happened—the shooting and the talking."

They picketed their horses—Ike said it was an insult to good cow ponies to call the three "crow-baits" by that name—and started for the cavern. But they had no sooner entered it than they became aware that it was inhabited, at least by a voice.

Out of the depths, in which showed a glow from either a lantern or a candle some distance in, echoed a pleading voice:

"Help! Help! Don't leave me alone this way! Help!"

Something like an electric shock went through Nat Ridley. He uttered an exclamation, drew his powerful flashlight from his pocket, and ran back into the cave, while the cowboys, after a startled look at each other, followed.

"Miss Ardell—Cora!" cried Nat. "Is that you? Are you here?"

"Yes! Yes! I am! Oh, is that Mr. Ridley? Thank heaven you have come to save me! Oh, help me!"

"That's just what we'll do, lady!" declared Slim.

"Surest thing you know!" added Ike, and both cowboys began rearranging their neckerchiefs, though the cave was too dark, even with the glow of a lantern and Nat's flashlight, to show any personal adornments.

"This must be the girl the sleuth was telling about," murmured Ike to Slim.

"That's right—the one kidnapped in Paloma. He sure is playing in great luck!"

Cora Ardell it was, a bound prisoner in the black cave. Nat Ridley soon freed her of the bonds.

"What happened and how did you get here?" asked the detective, when the girl had been given water to drink and led to a seat on a rude, wooden bench.

"That night after you came in late at the Paloma boarding house," related Cora when she had recovered her composure, "I fell asleep. I was awakened by feeling a hand over my mouth. I tried to get up, to scream, and to fight my assailant, but I was not able. I guess they had drugged me. I remember dimly that they asked me certain questions and that I answered, though I don't know what I said.

"Then they made me walk with them out of the house—two men in masks. It was as if I was in a daze. I dimly remember being put into an automobile, and then I came to my senses in this cave. I have been a prisoner here ever since, and the men have taken turns in demanding that I sign papers giving them back the oil wells."

"Did you?" asked Nat.

105

"I did not! They said they would kill me unless I signed, but I said my friends would rescue me. There were a number of men in this cave all the while. I think it must be the headquarters of the Tola gang."

"It begins to look so," admitted Nat. "But they must have only recently taken over this place, for you saw no signs of them when you two were here before, did you?" he asked the cowboys, and they answered in the negative.

"The other day," went on Cora, "there seemed to be a sudden alarm. All the men rushed out and I was left alone with an old Mexican and his wife. He has been my jailer ever since. I must say he did not treat me cruelly, though he kept me bound. Then the woman went away this morning, and I did not know what to think. A little while ago I heard horses approaching."

"They must have been our nags," remarked Ike. "And that rush the other day was after us."

"Yes," assented Nat. "Well, what happened then, Miss Ardell?"

"My Mexican guard suddenly rushed out a little while ago," the girl reported, "and then I began to work the gag from my mouth. I heard shots, and I struggled to free myself and shouted for help. Then you came in."

"I'm glad we did," replied Nat Ridley emphatically. "Your guard is out of the way," and he told something of what had happened. "The gang of Tolas left this cave to chase us," he went on. "But we gave them the slip and got back here by a roundabout way. They haven't returned yet, it seems."

"And will we be here when they come moseying in?" asked Ike.

"Not if I know it!" declared Slim. "I don't like the looks of their double daggers!"

"No, we sha'n't stay here," decided Nat Ridley. He had quickly made up his mind to a daring plan for rounding up the Tola gang, now that he had in his possession one of their double daggers.

"With your help, my cowboy friends," said the detective, "I'll have these scoundrels just where I want them. Can I count on you?"

"You bet!" came fervently from the pair.

"Then," said Nat Ridley in a low voice, "this is what I intend to do."

CHAPTER XXIII

THE DEAF MUTE

Within the silence of the dark cave, where, for days, Cora Ardell had been kept a prisoner, a secret conference was held. All the talk was in whispers, for Ike and Jim declared that they did not know enough about the cavern to insure that a listener might not be hidden in some recess.

It was even suggested that perhaps the Mexican whom Nat had shot twice might have sneaked back in an endeavor to get revenge, or, failing in this, to learn something of the plans of his enemies.

"We can't be too careful," whispered Nat, and so the low talk went on.

Following this conference, Ike hurried from the cave and went to a Mexican farmer whom he knew and purchased food with Nat's money, for the sleuth had come over the line well supplied financially. Cora, after the nerve-racking ordeal of being a prisoner had ended, became herself, and told much that she had overheard while bound in the cave.

That the cave was one of the headquarters of the dreaded Tola gang was well established, and it was only by chance that the two cowboys had not encountered the ruthless El Capitan Martolo, Don Castro and their followers on the visits Ike and Jim had paid to the cavern.

"Well, then," remarked Nat Ridley, one afternoon, about two days after the shooting of the double dagger from the hand of the Mexican who would have stabbed Slim Jim, "I'll leave you three for a while. Take good care of Miss Ardell," he warned the cowboys.

"We will," promised Ike.

"I'm not worrying a bit," the girl said.

"And we'll be on the lookout to join you," added Jim.

They watched the detective ride down the trail and out of sight.

While the cowboys were carrying out their promise to guard Cora Ardell carefully, quite a different scene was taking place in the Mexican village of Paz, some miles from Rolamotaza.

In a Mexican saloon, combined with which was a gambling joint, seated around a table in a rear room were El Capitan, Don Juan Castro, Valdez and a number of the other members of the secret society known as the Tola—an offshoot of some of the terrible organizations of the Aztec days. The talk was all in Spanish.

"It seems then," remarked the big El Capitan, "that our men did not get the American detective pig?"

"He escaped, to our sorrow," remarked Don Castro, who was telling the story.

"How?" snapped El Capitan.

"He and his cowboy companions abandoned their horses and lowered themselves over a cliff. We could not follow."

"How was that? Why not?" demanded El Capitan, his eyes blazing.

Don Castro shrugged his shoulders and waved his hands expressively as he replied:

"They pulled the ropes away so we could not slide down."

"Imbeciles!" snarled El Capitan. "Why did you not have ropes?"

"It was a mistake not to," admitted the leader of the baffled pursuers. "But we had none. However, we still have the girl in the dark cave, and it will be strange if she can hold out much longer. If she signs the papers, giving us back the oil wells, we can snap our fingers at this dog and pig of a Gringo detective."

"Perhaps," said El Capitan. "But he is very clever. Out of my pocket from under my nose he took letters—letters that say too much. Tell me," he went on with a change of manner. "Have you tortured the girl yet?"

"No, El Capitan," answered the other. "We did not know you wanted to go to that length."

"Go to any length! Do anything to get her to sign those papers. It is my order. Use hot irons if necessary. Now go and don't come back without the papers! Are you sure you have the girl safe?"

"Positive, El Capitan."

"That is good. We shall yet laugh at this pig of a Gringo."

El Capitan chuckled and ordered another drink, and while he was pouring it down his throat a waiter glided to his side and whispered in his ear.

"So?" exclaimed the Tola leader. "One of our band from the mountains to join us? Who is he? Does he bear the symbol?"

"He gave me this," and the waiter held out a card on which was drawn the device of a double dagger.

"That is good, but it is not enough. He should have the weapon itself, either in miniature or the large one. But I will see him. Don Castro, your attention here before you go to the cave on your mission," and El Capitan beckoned to his lieutenant.

"Yes, El Capitan," submissively responded the other. "What is it?"

"One of our band—or at least one so claiming—waits outside. He sends in his card. He is from the mountains it seems. He may be Pedro from the cave."

"If he is, it means that something has happened!" cried Don Castro, starting. His manner was alarming.

"You mean the girl has escaped?" hissed El Capitan.

"It is possible."

"If she has, you imbecile, I will hold you responsible!" stormed the leader. "But let us see! Have in this member from the mountains. He sends the proper card but he must have the dagger itself. Let him come in," he ordered the waiter.

A moment later an aged Mexican entered the meeting room of the Tola gang. White was his hair, bent was his back and he walked with a staff. He bowed humbly as he advanced and seemed eager to please as he stood before El Capitan.

"Who are you and what do you want?" snapped out the leader.

The old man appeared not to hear, and something in his manner caused El Capitan to exclaim:

"We are betrayed! This is a spy! Speak!" he cried, slipping his hand into his coat as if seeking a weapon.

"Pardon, señor, I forgot to mention that he is a deaf mute," said the waiter. "He had to write out on a card that he wanted to see you, and I had to write that I would take him your message and the symbol, which I did. He can neither hear nor speak."

"Fool, why did you not say so at first?" snarled El Capitan. "I had nearly put a bullet through him, and that would have been sad if he is really one of us. Look you," he went on to the stranger who stood meekly before him, "why do you come? What do you want?"

"You forget, El Capitan," said Don Castro, gently, "that he cannot hear you."

"True enough," grumbled the head of the gang. "Give me paper and pencil!"

"Make sure that he is one of us," suggested Don Castro.

"Am I not doing that?" testily inquired his chief.

He wrote something on a card which the deaf mute read, though slowly, either as if his eyesight were poor or his brain slow to comprehend. But comprehend he must have, for with a smile and a mumbling of sounds that were not words, he drew from his pocket a curiously carved handle.

Pressure on a certain ugly head among the decorations caused two keen blades to shoot out—one long and the other short.

"The double dagger!" murmured several who had crowded about El Capitan.

"Yes, he bears the emblem," admitted the chief. "He is one of us. But it is going to be devilish hard to get much out of him. I hate writing. However, I will see what his mission is."

But hardly had El Capitan begun to frame some questions in writing than there rushed into the meeting room a Mexican with a hand done up in bandages, and with but a bloody smear where, once, an ear had been.

"Pedro!" gasped Don Castro. "Pedro!"

"From the cave?" El Capitan.

"From the cave!" answered the wounded Tola. "They shot me and they have the girl!!"

"Ten thousand devils!" yelled El Capitan. "Speak! Who has the girl? What do you mean? Who? Tell me! We are lost!"

He started forward as though to seize the messenger and shake the truth from him, but Don Castro stepped forward, while the deaf mute, putting the double dagger, in which the two blades were once more sheathed, back in his pocket, drew quietly into a corner.

"Let me talk to Pedro," suggested Don Castro. "What happened to you and who took the girl?" he asked quietly.

Then followed a flood of talk, hearing which El Capitan yelled:

"It is that dog of an Americano detective again. Always he turns up un-expectedly. He must die! Quick, call in Valdez and Latro. Set the killers on his trail! He must die! Dog! Pig! Thus to baffle us!"

"He must die!" echoed Don Castro, a wicked smile playing over his face. "But to kill him we must first catch him, and I think Pedro will help. Let us go into conference. And what of this deaf and dumb member from the mountain, El Capitan?"

"His matter can wait. He can hear nothing—tell nothing. Let him wait," and he made a sign to the aged Mexican who had shown the double dagger to take a seat in the corner whither he had retreated, there to wait until the more important matter of planning Nat Ridley's death could be disposed of.

The deaf mute sat down wearily, as though he had traveled far, and he closed his eyes. But there was a curious little smile playing over his brown and wrinkled face.

CHAPTER XXIV

OVER THE LINE

Late into the night, yes, almost until the red sun was ready to rise and shine down into the village of Paz amid the Mexican hills, did El Capitan, Don Castro, Pedro and the "killers" hold conference in the back room of the adobe saloon. Now the voices were high pitched and now they were low, and all the while the deaf mute sat in his corner, nodding, sleeping, and sometimes smiling.

At last a plan was agreed upon and certain men of the company girded their pistol belts tighter about them. They were given money by El Capitan and then they went out into the gray and reddening dawn to where their horses awaited.

"Fail not!" ordered the big chief. "The son of Gringo pig must die!"

"He shall die!" promised Latro, with a cruel smile on his face. "We shall meet with our comrades in Paloma and it will be strange if, between us, we shall not find him."

"In Paloma, then, I will join you on the day agreed," said El Capitan.

Again the brown and wrinkled deaf mute in his corner smiled. Then the leader seemed to remember the mute messenger with the double dagger, for he turned to Don Castro and said:

"Now we shall see what he wants. A pest upon him for coming at such a time! It is money he desires, I doubt not."

And money was just what the aged member of the Tola gang had come for. It appeared, from what he wrote down on dirty pieces of paper, that he was a member of a distant branch of the gang that had its headquarters in the mountains. It was composed of poor peons, but they had been promised a share in the oil wells, the profits of which were to be divided among the Tolas.

It further appeared that El Capitan, Don Castro and the others, not having sufficient funds of their own to wrest back from the Lemberg family the wonderfully profitable wells, had levied contributions from every member of the gang, rich and poor, promising in return money when the wells should once more be owned by the ancient society.

"And this fellow says he and his fellow villagers are so poor from the failure of their crops and because of the money they have given us to get back our wells that they are starving," said El Capitan when he had read what the deaf mute wrote. "A pest upon them! Why could they not wait?" He walked the floor in anger.

"What is to be done?" asked Don Castro.

"What would you have?" retorted El Capitan. "We cannot afford disaffection. These mountain members, though they add little to our success, must still be considered. But I am tired of this pencil scratching, Castro. You deal with this mute. Write him that if he will wait a few days he shall have money to take to his friends. By that time we shall have our wells back."

"If we get the girl and kill that devil of a detective—maybe," added Don Castro, with a shrug of his shoulders.

"We will!" declared the leader. "Deal you, Castro, with our member from the mountains. Pacify him—tell him to wait and all will be well."

"I suppose he is a member," suggested the other.

"Did he not have the double dagger? Who else but a member would dare show it? He is a true Tola. Treat him well. And now we shall hope for the best. I am weary—I would sleep!"

So while El Capitan staggered off to his room, Don Castro wrote more messages to the deaf mute who read them slowly—and smiled.

It was several days after this, during which time El Capitan, together with several of his most trusted men, had departed on a mission, that Don Castro, sauntering one day into the café headquarters of the Tola gang, inquired for Zenna, which, the deaf mute had written, was his name.

"He is gone," the café proprietor answered.

"Gone?"

"Yes. He left in the night. Someone came to him with a note and he departed hurriedly. Why? Was I supposed to detain him? Is all not right?"

"I don't know about the last," said Don Castro slowly. "I hope so. Certainly you had no orders to detain him. I wonder if he was a Tola."

"He had the double dagger," replied the café owner, who was also one of the ruthless gang. "I saw him springing the blades in and out as he sat here early in the evening."

"Yes, he had the double dagger," agreed Don Castro. "But I wonder—I wonder!" Then, with a shrug of his shoulders he added: "But El Capitan said he was one of us, and El Capitan should know."

Meanwhile the bent and aged deaf mute was making good time over the mountain trails on the mule that had brought him to the village of Paz. And, as he hastened forward, now and then he took out the double dagger and looked at it. Ever and anon he smiled, wrinkling his bronzed face.

* * * *

In a little adobe hut, long and narrow, several men were gathered one hot, sultry evening. Two of the party were cowboys, by their dress. One spoke in slow, drawling tones and moved but seldom. The other was tall and slim.

Two others of the party were evidently Easterners, as their pale faces, in contrast to the bronzed complexions of their companions, plainly showed.

"Well, Baldy," remarked one of these latter, "we're a long, long way from Times Square."

"You said it, Berry!" responded the other. "But this is the place the chief told us to report to, isn't it?"

"You got it right, gentlemen," said the tall, thin cowboy. "Me an' Lazy Ike doped this out as the best place to pull off the party; didn't we, Ike?" he asked his companion who had gone into another part of the long, low building which was divided in the middle by a partition containing a door. "Where's Ike?" he asked, looking at Baldy and Berry.

"I crossed over into Mexico to get me a match for my cigarette," answered Lazy Ike, coming through the door. "Now I'm in the U. S. A. once more," he went on as he sat down with the others.

"Is it true?" asked Baldy Stoler of Slim Burke, "that this building is right over the line between the United States and Mexico?"

"You got it right, buddy," was the answer. "It was built for a saloon, after prohibition started, so liquor could be sold to thirsty United Staters who didn't want to go into Mexico. They could come in here and imbibe and still be on Uncle Sam's land. In case of a raid the red-eye and forty-rod could be hustled over to the other side of the saloon, on to Mexican territory, and the prohibition people couldn't do a thing. It got so, after a while, that the United States authorities and the Mexican government made an agreement and this place was wiped out by a joint raid. Since then this shack is in charge of the military authorities of both countries."

"And when Nat telephoned Baldy and me to come here," said Berry, "and when we met you two cowboys, you said this was the best place for the trick."

"It is," asserted Slim Jim. "It's just over the line, you see."

Others in the crowd listened to this talk. Hard-fisted men they were, and ready with their guns. Baldy looked at his watch and remarked:

"It's about time he was here if he's coming."

At that moment a door in the Mexican end of the building opened and an old man shuffled in. Bent and wrinkled he was, and stained and dusty from long travel.

"What do you want?" called Ike sharply. "Who are you?"

"Excuse me, señor, but I am deaf and dumb," was the reply.

For a moment this remarkable statement seemed to shock them all into silence, and then Berry Todd laughed and cried:

"It's the chief himself—Nat Ridley!"

"Hush!" cautioned the detective, for he it was. "They are on the way. They will soon be here. Into the other room with you—the United States side and wait for my whistle. Have your guns ready."

"That's something we won't have nothin' else but," declared Lazy Ike with his characteristic drawl.

A little later the aged Mexican seemed to be alone in the long, narrow building that straddled the international line. He sat in a chair, waiting, waiting, with a queer smile on his brown face.

Presently he heard the sound of horses ambling along the road, and the smile changed to a stern expression. He rose as several men opened the door and came in, El Capitan and Don Castro among them.

"He is here!" exclaimed the leader, glancing at the Mexican. "I thought he was one of us, though you doubted him, Don Castro. Now then, somebody, write and ask him where he has the girl and that pig of a detective. I must have a drink," and El Capitan drew out a flask while Don Castro wrote the questions of his chief on a piece of paper which he handed the old Mexican, who had appointed this rendezvous after his sudden flight from Paz.

But the deaf mute seemed to have some difficulty in reading the writing. He held it up beneath a candle spluttering in a wall sconce. And, as he raised his arms, Don Castro gave a cry of alarm.

"What is it?" cried El Capitan, nearly choking himself as he stopped his drink half taken. "What is it?"

"We are betrayed!" shouted Don Castro. "See! This man is no peon! He is in disguise! His skin is stained! I doubted him from the first. Now I am sure!"

With a quick motion Don Castro pulled back the sleeve from the upraised arm of the man reading the note. And while the hand and wrist were stained a mahogany brown, the remainder of the arm was glistening white skin.

"Son of a pig!" hissed El Capitan as, from an inner pocket, he drew his double dagger and sprang toward Nat Ridley.

CHAPTER XXV

THE WHISTLE

Thought was hardly quicker than Nat Ridley's act as he pulled loose his sleeve from the betraying grip of Don Castro and leaped toward the door dividing the long building in two. As he glided from the grasp of the Mexican, the latter gave a cry of dismay.

"After him!" shouted El Capitan. "He must not escape again! He knows too much!"

"Devil of a spy!" cried some of the other Tolas who, with their leaders, had come over into the United States in furtherance of their plans and because of certain things the deaf mute had written in his notes. The mute had promised to deliver into their hands Nat Ridley the detective, and to tell where Cora Ardell could be found.

"Spy! Spy!" yelled the baffled and enraged Mexicans, while El Capitan seemed actually to foam at the mouth.

"He said he would deliver Ridley to us!" cried Don Castro.

"And he is here!" cried the ringing voice of the supposed deaf mute. "Nat Ridley is here! Come and get him! I am Nat Ridley, at your service!"

He leaped into the other room, which appeared to be vacant. After him rushed El Capitan, Don Castro and the "killers." Each one held either a double dagger or a gun.

For a moment it seemed that Nat Ridley would be either killed or captured. But the same smile that had wrinkled the brown face of the supposed Mexican now corrugated that of the sleuth and he shouted:

"Come in and get me!"

Into the room—occupied only by the detective it seemed—rushed the Tola gang.

Then Nat Ridley put a whistle to his lips and blew a shrill blast. Instantly certain boxes along the sides of the room were shoved aside and there appeared two cowboys and Baldy Stoler and Berry Todd and a number of United States revenue officers, each one grim of face and holding two guns.

"Betrayed! Betrayed!" snarled Don Castro.

"All is not lost yet!" shouted El Capitan. "We are on Mexican soil. These pigs of Americanos cannot arrest us!"

"There's where you're wrong!" cried Nat Ridley, his hand in his coat pocket. "You're on United States soil. There's the international line!" and he pointed to a black mark running along the floor just where the door was set in the partition. "You're in the United States and you're all prisoners!" his voice rang out. "This is the end of the Tola gang!"

"Not yet!" snarled El Capitan. "The double dagger will be avenged!"

He leaped at Nat with the two-pointed knife he drew from his coat, but as he sprang there was a sharp report, a puff of smoke from the detective's pocket, and El Capitan crumpled up on the floor, a bullet through his heart.

"It is my turn!" yelled Don Castro.

He drew his gun and aimed at Nat from behind. But Berry Todd saw the motion and the detective's gun spoke once. Don Castro went down, the bullet striking him in the mouth as he opened it to yell his defiance.

Several of the Mexicans began firing, but they were poor shots and the bullets flew wild, while the guns of the cowboys, the three detectives, and those of the revenue officers did fearful execution. Several of the Tola gang were killed, and the others, in a panic of fear, threw down their weapons, raised their hands in the air, and cried out that they surrendered.

"Well, then, I guess this is about all," remarked Nat Ridley as the cowed wretches were led away to the Paloma jail, the fight having taken place on the outskirts of the city. "Is Miss Ardell all right?" he went on. "Where is she?"

"You can see for yourself," remarked Slim Jim. He went to a side door, opened it, and Cora entered.

* * * *

So ended the reign of terror instituted by the Tolas when they found that the oil wells were more valuable than had been supposed. With the leaders slain and most of the principals in jail, the order was all but wiped out. In some ways it was a lawful secret society, and there were good members of it, particularly in the mountains among the poor and honest peons.

But the Tola had been corrupted by El Capitan for his own ends and those of his friends, and the forcing of the oil wells from the Lembergs, who were lawfully entitled to them, was only part of their plans.

Nat Ridley had learned all their secrets while in their headquarters disguised as the deaf and dumb Mexican. He learned how the deaths of the three Lembergs had been brought about, and from the persons of the slain and captured men were taken several large double daggers and a number of the small ones, with the drugged points—emblems used to strike terror to the hearts of the enemies of the Tolas.

"Dan Steele is avenged," said Nat when, having resumed his own character, he was ready to go back to New York with Berry and Baldy.

"And my cousins' widows and the other heirs will be in undisputed possession of their oil wells," added Cora Ardell. "My own interests will also be safe now, thanks to you," she said to Nat with a grateful smile.

They were soon on their way north in a train, for the girl decided that she had had enough of Mexico. Certain trusted agents were left in charge of the oil-well property.

"And when will you send in your bill?" asked Cora presently.

"What bill?" came from Nat, wonderingly.

"The bill for your services," said the girl. "I want to pay my share, and I know, my cousins' widows will also. How much do we owe you?"

"Nothing at all," was the prompt answer. "What I did was done to rid the country of a desperate gang and to avenge my friend Dan Steele. It wasn't a question of money. I don't want a reward. Dan Steele is avenged!"

"Good and plenty!" echoed Baldy Stoler.

And then Nat Ridley settled back in his seat for a well-deserved rest.

THE END

www.ingramcontent.com/pod-product-compliance
Lightning Source LLC
Chambersburg PA
CBHW010932120626
46552CB00009B/3230